THE AUSTRALIAN CLASSICS LIBRARY

The Moods of Ginger Mick

C.J. Dennis

Introduction by Philip Butterss

General editors

Bruce Bennett, University of New South Wales

Robert Dixon, University of Sydney

SYDNEY UNIVERSITY PRESS

Published 2009 by Sydney University Press

SYDNEY UNIVERSITY PRESS

Fisher Library, University of Sydney
www.sup.usyd.edu.au

First published in 1916 by Angus & Robertson, Sydney

This, the Australian Classics Library text of *The Moods of Ginger Mick* is a repaging of text files on SETIS, themselves input from the 1916 edition published by Angus & Robertson, Sydney

© Introduction by Philip Butterss 2009

© Sydney University Press 2009

The publication of this book is part of the University of Sydney Library's Australian Studies electronic texts initiative. Further details are available at:
www.sup.usyd.edu.au/oztexts/

Front cover image: portrait of C.J. Dennis, 1889. Courtesy of the National Library of Australia

ISBN   978-1-920898-98-4

Designed and printed in Australia at the University Publishing Service, University of Sydney

Contents

Introduction

Ginger Mick, the larrikin hero of Gallipoli, was a household name during World War I. The first edition of C.J. Dennis's *The Moods of Ginger Mick*, released on 9 October 1916, ran to almost 40,000 copies—an astonishing figure for a book of verse (McLaren, 115). Reviews were warm, though not quite as effusive as those for its predecessor, *The Songs of a Sentimental Bloke*. The *Bulletin* described *The Moods of Ginger Mick* as 'finely patriotic' and 'uniquely Australian' (19 October 1916), while the *Argus* gushed about its author's talents: 'Mr. Dennis uses slang as a flexible medium, constructing subtle epigrams with it, expressing deep philosophical truths with it, exciting mirth and sorrow with it, and writing lyrics in it (20 October 1916).' A second impression of 15,000 copies was issued on 1 November, and a trench edition for soldiers sold well. When it was published in London in December 1917, 63,000 copies had been printed (McLaren, 115).

This larrikin soldier had his origins in March 1913 in a poem published in the *Bulletin*. Dennis wanted to refer in passing to the Sentimental Bloke's gambling partner, and Ginger Mick was born as a convenient rhyme to 'shick' (Chisholm, 64). As Dennis added poems to this series that was ultimately to become *The Songs of a Sentimental Bloke*, Mick reappeared as best man at the Bloke's wedding, where he is identified as a rabbit-seller: he extols the virtues of the bride, Doreen, and embarrasses the groom in a short speech. In another episode, he leads the newly married groom astray, taking him out drinking and gambling all night.

The Moods of Ginger Mick, written in the same larrikinese as *The Songs of a Sentimental Bloke*, is usually regarded as Dennis response to the phenomenal success of the earlier volume, published in October 1915.

Actually, though, he began seriously developing the character earlier than this, publishing 'The Call of Stoush', the first poem devoted to Mick (and originally named 'Ginger Mick'), in the *Bulletin* in June 1915. By the time the Bloke book appeared, five of the 16 chapters of *The Moods of Ginger Mick* were already in print.

In dating his introduction 25 April 1916, the first anniversary of the landing at Gallipoli, Dennis was offering *The Moods of Ginger Mick* as a memorial to the Anzacs and, at the same time, cashing in on popular sentiment. The main outline of the Anzac legend was powerfully articulated and widely disseminated through the verses about Mick's feats in the Dardanelles, and also through *The Anzac Book*, edited by C.E.W. Bean and published in the same year. For audiences at home, Dennis's volume depicts Mick as representative of all Australian fighting men: what he did, 'a thousand uv 'is cobbers would 'ave done' (64). And the values expressed in *The Moods of Ginger Mick* include courage, mateship, nationalism and sacrifice. Absent is the anti-British feeling that is today an important strand of the Anzac story. Instead, Dennis verse sets out what Ken Inglis has described as 'a legend in which Australians were still loyal to the Empire but mature enough to be full partners in it' (Inglis, 83). The book's conclusion, where 'an English toff wiv swanky friends' (63) declares that Mick was a 'gallant gentleman', gave the nation exactly what it had wanted at the start of the war: international and, most importantly, Imperial acknowledgement of Australians' worth as fighters and as men.

The Moods of Ginger Mick must be seen in the context of the Great War's shocking casualty lists: out of an Australian population of about five million, almost 420,000 enlisted; over 60,000 were killed, and more than 150,000 were wounded, gassed or taken prisoner. Almost everyone in the country was personally affected. For friends and families back home, the process of mourning was made more difficult by the fact that the bodies were not returned to Australia, and often telegrams contained no more information than that a loved one was missing, believed killed. Mourners were comforted by British high cultural poetry such as Lawrence Binyon's

'For the Fallen' and Rupert Brookes's 'The Dead'. Dennis's popular verse was also helpful for Australian audiences, providing them with a heady emotional cocktail, principally of pride, grief and laughter. At the same time, he was acutely aware of his readers' ambivalence about the outpouring of emotion, and was careful periodically to undercut any unseemly excess.

The public responded strongly, much to the disgust of Norman Lindsay, who found the popularity of Dennis's work proof of his compatriots' inability to think and feel deeply. He wrote in 1917, 'the damnable fact is patent that all over Australia people read *Ginger Mick*, and *The Sentimental Bloke*, and find the maudlin rubbish a consolation for their dead' (*Letters*, 98). Among Lindsay's own consolations, however, was a belief that a ouija board communicated messages from his brother Reg, who was killed at the Somme (Inglis, 104).

The Moods of Ginger Mick was released into a profoundly divided society three weeks before the first referendum on conscription. The book makes no mention of that debate, and is vague about Mick's reason for enlisting, saying only that he felt 'the Call uv Stoush' (18), an ancient and evidently unexplainable impulse deep within men. It more deliberately addresses class division in Australian culture, with its overall structure and several of its episodes depicting a transition from class antagonism to unity between those of all backgrounds. On a number of occasions, Mick discovers that nationalism—'Pride o' Race'—is more important than 'pride o' class', and although he is not assigned any denomination, Ginger Mick may have taken on a new relevance in the context of sectarian tension. In the middle of the conscription debates, and after the Dublin uprising in Easter 1916, assertions of comradeship between all Australians may have had an added dimension when made by one whose name suggested Irish Catholic descent.

The illustrations were by Hal Gye, Dennis's close friend, whose whimsical portrayals of larrikins as cupids were so important to *The Songs of a Sentimental Bloke*'s gentle appeal. Here, the demands of a volume about war required a different male image. For the sequel, as Gye records, there could be 'nothing of the cupid touch; they had to be of men—real men; and yet, as Den said, to be drawn lightly' (Gye, 62). The earlier book had been centrally concerned with how men should behave; as its title indicates, it explores an accommodation between being a bloke and being 'sentimental'. *The Moods of Ginger Mick* portrays soldiers, but it is also at pains to show they can have deep feeling. The volume reassures readers that beneath its hero's tough exterior is 'a big, soft-'earted boy' (5); in its examination of his love for Rose, it demonstrates Mick's potential to be a good husband and father; and it suggests that soldiers will be able to be reintegrated into Australian society after the war.

The Moods of Ginger Mick did not achieve the long-lasting fame of its predecessor. Some of the attitudes about race are unacceptable today, and this is also true of 'The Battle of the Wazzir', a poem celebrating the riotous behaviour of Australian troops in Egypt that was rejected by the censor. Dennis had intended it to sit between 'The Push' and 'Sari Bair'; it was published separately in the *Bulletin* of 18 July 1918. In 1920 a silent film version, *Ginger Mick*, directed by Raymond Longford and using the stars from his *Sentimental Bloke* (1919), was released to acclaim. After the war the Australian public was glad to turn its attention to other matters, and the book's popularity waned, although well-thumbed copies remained in many households for generations.

Philip Butterss

University of Adelaide

References

Butterss, Philip. 'C.J. Dennis (1876–1938).' In Samuels, Selina, ed. *Australian Writers, 1915–1950*. Detroit, Michigan: Gale Group, 2002. 81–87.

Chisholm, Alec H. *The Making of a Sentimental Bloke: A Sketch of the Remarkable Career of C.J. Dennis*. Melbourne: Georgian House, 1946.

Gye, Hal. 'The story of C.J. Dennis.' Papers of C.J. Dennis and Hal Gye, National Library of Australia, MS 6480/100.

Herron, Margaret. *Down the Years*. Melbourne: Hallcraft, 1953.

Howarth, R.G. and Barker A.W., eds. *Letters of Norman Lindsay*. Sydney: Angus & Robertson, 1979.

Inglis, K.S. *Sacred Places: War Memorials in the Australian Landscape*. Melbourne: Melbourne University Press, 1998.

McLaren, Ian. *C.J. Dennis: A Comprehensive Bibliography Based on the Collection of the Compiler*. Adelaide: Libraries Board of South Australia, 1979.

McLaren, Ian F. *Talking about C.J. Dennis*. Melbourne: Monash University, 1982.

Watts, Barry, ed. *The World of the Sentimental Bloke*. Sydney: Angus & Robertson, 1976.

THE MOODS
OF GINGER MICK

BY

C. J. DENNIS

Author of '' The Songs of a Sentimental Bloke,'' etc.

With Illustrations by Hal Gye

SYDNEY
ANGUS & ROBERTSON LTD.
89 CASTLEREAGH STREET
1916

[Facsimile of first edition titlepage]

DEDICATED TO
THE BOYS WHO TOOK THE COUNT

INTRODUCTION

JIST to intrajuice me cobber, an' 'is name is Ginger Mick—
A rorty boy, a naughty boy, wiv rude ixpressions thick
In 'is casu'l conversation, an' the wicked sort o' face
That gives the sudden shudders to the lor-abidin' race.

'Is name is on the records at the Melbourne City Court,
Fer doin' things an' sayin' things no reel nice feller ort;
An' 'is name is on the records uv the Army, over there,
Fer doin' things—same sort o' things that rose the Bench's 'air.

They never rung no joy-bells when 'e made 'is first de-boo;
But 'e got free edjication, w'ich they fondly shoved 'im thro';
Then turned 'im loose in Spadger's Lane to 'ang around the street
An' 'elp the cop to re-erlize the 'ardness uv 'is beat.

Then 'e quickly dropped 'is aitches, so as not to be mistook
Fer an edjicated person, 'oo 'is cobbers reckoned crook;
But 'e 'ad a trick wiv figgers that ud make a clerk look sick;
So 'e pencilled fer a bookie; an' 'e 'awked a bit, did Mick.

A bloke can't be pertick'ler 'oo must battle fer a crust;
An' some, they pinch fer preference, an' some, becos they must.
When times is 'ard, an' some swell coves is richer than they ort;
Well, it's just a little gamble fer a rise, agin the Court.

Now, Mick wus never in it as a reel perfeshnal crook,
But sometimes cops 'as slabs uv luck, so sometimes 'e wus took,
An' 'e got a repitation, thro' 'im bein' twice interned;
But 'e didn't skite about it, 'cos 'e felt it wasn't earned.

I reckerlect one time a Beak slings Mick a slab uv guff,
Wiv "Thirty days or forty bob" (Mick couldn't raise the stuff)—
An' arsts 'im where 'is conshuns is, an' w'y 'e can't be good,
An' Mick jist grins, an' takes it out, an' never understood.

An' that is orl there wus to Mick, wiv orl 'is leery ways.
If I wus up among the 'eads, wiv right to blame or praise,
Whenever some sich bloke as 'im wus tucked away fer good
I'd chalk them words above 'is 'ead: " 'E never understood."

If I wus up among the 'eads, wiv right to judge the game,
I'd look around fer chance to praise, an' sling the flamin' blame;
Fer findin' things in blokes to praise pays divvies either way;
An' wot they're blamed fer yesterd'y brings 'earty cheers to-day.

Yes, 'earty cheers frum thortless coots 'oo feel dead sure their God
Would never 'ave no time fer crooks 'oo does a stretch in quod;
'Oo reckon 'eaven is a place where orl folk tork correck,
An' Judgment, where the "vulgar" gits it solid in the neck.

An' Ginger Mick wus vulgar. 'Struth! When things wus gettin' slow
'E took to 'awkin' rabbits, w'ich is very, very low—
'E wus the sort o' bloke to watch when 'e come in yer gate:
'E 'ad a narsty fightin' face that orl nice people 'ate.

'E 'ad that narsty fightin' face that peaceful folk call grim;
But I 'ave seen it grow reel soft when kiddies spoke to 'im.

'E 'ad them narsty sullen eyes that nice folk can't enjure;
But I 'ave seen a smile in 'em that made our frien'ship sure.

There's men 'oo never knoo ole Mick, an' passed 'im in the street,
An' looks away an' sez, "See 'im? A narsty chap to meet!
'E'd be an ugly customer alone an' after dark!"
An' Mick, 'e'd twitch 'is jor at 'em, 'arf earnest, 'arf a lark.

That wus the sort o' character that Mick earned be 'is looks.
The talk uv 'im, the walk uv 'im, put 'im among the crooks.
An' Mick, 'e looks on swank an' style as jist a lot o' flam,
An' snouted them that snouted 'im, an' never give a dam.

But spite uv orl 'is 'ulkin' frame, an' langwidge flowin' free,
I seen the thing inside uv Mick that made 'im good to me.
An' spite uv orl the sneerin' ways that leery blokes imploy,
I knoo 'im jist fer wot 'e wus—a big, soft-'earted boy.

Fer when a bloke 'as come to be reel cobbers wiv a bloke,
They sorter swap good fellership wivout words bein' spoke.
I never slung no guff to Mick, 'e never smooged to me,
But we could smoke, an' 'old our jor, an' be reel company.

There 'as bin times that 'e would curse to 'ave recalled by me,
When I 'ave seen 'im doin' things that coves calls charity;
An' there's been times, an' frequent times, in spite uv orl 'is looks,
When I 'ave 'eard 'im sayin' things that blokes shoves inter books.

But Ginger Mick wus Ginger Mick—a leery boy, fer keeps,
'Oo 'owled "Wile Rabbee!" in the streets, in tones that give yeh creeps.
'E never planned 'is mode uv life, nor chose the Lane fer lair,
No more than 'e designed 'is chiv or colour uv 'is 'air.

So Ginger 'awked, an' Ginger pinched, an' Ginger went to quod,
An' never thort to waste 'is time in blamin' man or God—
An' then there came the Call uv Stoush, or Jooty—wot's a name?
An' Ginger cocked 'is ear to it, an' found 'is flamin' game.

I intrajuice me cobber 'ere; an' don't make no ixcuse
To any culchered click that it's a peb I intrajuice.
I dunno wot 'is ratin' wus in this 'ere soshul plan;
I only know, inside o' me, I intrajuice a man.

MELBOURNE, THE SENTIMENTAL BLOKE
April 25th, 1916.

DUCK AN' FOWL

NOW, when a bloke 'e cracks a bloke fer insults to a skirt,
    An' wrecks a joint to square a lady's name,
They used to call it chivalry, but now they calls it dirt,
    An' the end of it is cops an' quod an' shame.
Fer insults to fair Gwendoline they 'ad to be wiped out;
But Rosie's sort is jist fair game—when Ginger ain't about.

It wus Jimmie Ah Foo's cook-shop, which is close be Spadger's Lane,
    Where a vari'gated comp'ny tears the scran,
An' there's some is "tup'ny coloured," an' some is "penny plain,"
    Frum a lawyer to a common lumper-man.
Or a writer fer the papers, or a slaver on the prowl,
An' noiseless Chows a-glidin' 'round wiv plates uv duck an' fowl.

But if yeh wanted juicy bits that 'ung around Foo's perch
    Yeh fetched 'em down an' wolfed 'em in yer place.
An' Foo sat sad an' solim, like an 'oly man in church,
    Wiv an early-martyr look upon 'is face;
Wot never changed, not even when a toff upon a jag
Tried to pick up Ginger's Rosie, an' collided wiv a snag.

Ginger Mick's bin at the races, an' 'e'd made a little rise,
    'Avin' knowed a bloke wot knowed the trainer's cook.
An' easy money's very sweet, as punters reckernise,
    An' sweetest when yeh've prized it orf a "book."

So Ginger calls fer Rosie, an' to celerbrate 'is win
'E trots 'er down to Ah Foo's joint to splash a bit uv tin.

There wus lights, an' smells of Asia, an' a strange, Chow-'aunted scene;
    Floatin' scraps of forrin lingo 'it the ear;
But Rose sails in an' takes 'er seat like any soshul queen
    Sich as stokes 'erself wiv foy grass orl the year.
"Duck an' Fowl" 's 'er nomination; so ole Ginger jerks 'is frame
'Cross to git some fancy pickin's, an' to give 'is choice a name.

While Ginger paws the tucker, an' 'as words about the price,
    There's a shickered toff slings Rosie goo-goo eyes.
'E's a mug 'oo thinks 'e's 'it a flamin' 'all uv scarlet vice
    An' 'e picks on gentle Rosie fer a prize.
Then 'e tries to play at 'andies, an' arrange about a meet;
But Rosie fetches 'im a welt that shifts 'im in 'is seat.

Ginger's busy makin' bargins, an' 'e never seen the clout;
    'E is 'agglin' wiv Ah Foo fer 'arf a duck;
But the toff's too shick or silly fer to 'eave 'is carkis out,
    An' to fade while goin's good an' 'e's in luck.
Then Ginger clinched 'is bargin, an', as down the room 'e came.
'E seen the toff jump frum 'is seat, an' call the girl a name.

That done it. Less than 'arf a mo, an' 'ell got orf the chain;
    An' the swell stopped 'arf a ducklin' wiv 'is neck,
As Ginger guv the war-cry that is dreaded in the Lane.
    An' the rest wus whirlin' toff an' sudden wreck.
Mick never reely stoushed 'im, but 'e used 'im fer a mop.
Then someone doused the bloomin' glim, an' Foo run fer a cop.

Down the stairs an' in the passidge come the shufflin' feet uv Chows,
    An' a crash, as Ah Foo's chiner found its mark.
Fer more than Mick 'ad ancient scores left over frum ole rows,

An' more than one stopped somethin' in the dark.
Then the tabbies took to screamin', an' a Chow remarked "Wha' for?"
While the live ducks quacked blue murder frum their corner uv the floor.

Fer full ten minutes it wus joy, reel willin' an' to spare,
    Wiv noise uv tarts, an' Chows, an' ducks, an' lash;
An' plates uv fowl an' bird's-nest soup went whizzin' thro' the air,
    While 'arf-a-dozen fought to reach Foo's cash.
Then, thro' an open doorway, three Chows' 'eads is framed in light,
An' sudden in Mick's corner orl is gentle peace an' quite.

Up goes the lights; in comes the cops; an' there's a sudden rush;
    But the Johns 'as got 'em safe an' 'emmed 'em in;
An' ev'ryone looks innercent. Then thro' the anxious 'ush
    The toff's voice frum the floor calls fer a gin …
But Mick an' Rose, O where are they? Arst uv the silent night!
They 'ad a date about a dawg, an' vanished out o' sight.

Then Foo an' orl 'is cousins an' the ducks torks orl at once,
    An' the tabbies pitch the weary Johns a tale,
'Ow they orl is puffick ladies 'oo 'ave not bin pinched fer munce;
    An' the crooks does mental sums concernin' bail.
The cops they takes a name er two, then gathers in the toff,
An' lobs 'im in a cold, 'ard cell to sleep 'is love-quest off.

But down in Rosie's kipsie, at the end uv Spadger's Lane,
    'Er an' Mick is layin' supper out fer two.
"Now, I 'ate the game," sez Ginger, "an' it goes agin the grain;
    But wot's a 'elpless, 'ungry bloke to do?"
An' 'e yanks a cold roast chicken frum the bosom uv 'is shirt,
An' Rosie finds a ducklin' underneath 'er Sund'y skirt.

So, when a bloke fergits 'imself, an' soils a lady's name,
    Altho' Romance is dead an' in the dirt,

In ole Madrid or Little Bourke they treats 'im much the same,
　　An' 'e collects wot's comin' fer a cert.
But, spite uv 'igh-falutin' tork, the fact is jist the same:
Ole Ginger Mick wus out fer loot, an' played a risky game.

To fight an' forage … Spare me days! It's been man's leadin' soot
　　Since 'e learned to word a tart an' make a date.
'E's been at it, good an' solid, since ole Adam bit the froot:
　　To fight an' forage, an' pertect 'is mate.
But this story 'as no moral, an' it 'as a vulgar plot;
It is jist a small igzample uv a way ole Ginger's got.

WAR

'E SEZ to me, "Wot's orl this flamin' war?
    The papers torks uv nothin' else but scraps.
An' wot's ole England got snake-'eaded for?
    An' wot's the strength uv callin' out our chaps?"
'E sez to me, "Struth! Don't she rule the sea?
Wot does she want wiv us?" 'e sez to me.

Ole Ginger Mick is loadin' up 'is truck
    One mornin' in the markit feelin' sore.
'E sez to me, "Well, mate, I've done me luck;
    An' Rose is arstin', 'Wot about this war?'
I'm gone a tenner at the two-up school;
The game is crook, an' Rose is turnin' cool."

'E sez to me, " 'Ow is it fer a beer?"
    I tips 'im 'ow I've told me wife, Doreen,
That when I comes down to the markit 'ere
    I dodges pubs, an' chucks the tipple, clean.
Wiv 'er an' kid alone up on the farm
She's full uv fancies that I'll come to 'arm.

"'Enpecked!" 'e sez. An' then, "Ar, I dunno.
    I wouldn't mind if I wus in yer place.
I've 'arf a mind to give cold tea a go.
    It's no game, pourin' snake-juice in yer face.

But, lad, I 'ave to, wiv the thirst I got.
I'm goin' over now to stop a pot."

'E goes acrost to find a pint a 'ome;
    An' meets a pal an' keeps another down.
Ten minutes later, when 'e starts to roam
    Back to the markit, wiv an ugly frown,
'E sprags a soljer bloke 'oo's passin' by,
An' sez 'e'd like to dot 'im in the eye.

"Your sort," sez Mick, "don't know yer silly mind!
    They lead yeh like a sheep; it's time yeh woke—
The 'eads is makin' piles out uv your kind!"
    "Aw, git yer 'ead read!" sez the soljer bloke.
'Struth! 'e wus willin' wus that Kharki chap;
I 'ad me work cut out to stop a scrap.

An' as the soljer fades acrost the street,
    Mick strikes a light an' sits down on 'is truck,
An' chews 'is fag—a sign 'is nerve is beat—
    An' swears a bit, an' sez 'e's done 'is luck.
'E grouches there ten minutes, maybe more,
Then sez quite sudden, *Blarst the flamin' war!*"

Jist then a motor car goes glidin' by
    Wiv two fat toffs be'ind two fat cigars.
Mick twigs 'em frum the corner uv 'is eye.
    "I 'ope," 'e sez, "the 'Uns don't git my cars.
Me di'mon's, too, don't let me sleep a wink …
Ar, 'Struth! I'd fight fer that sort—I *don't* think."

'E sits there while I 'arness up me prad,
    Chewin' 'is fag an' starin' at the ground.
I tumbles that 'e's got the joes reel bad,

An' don't say nothin' till 'e comes around.
'E sez 'is luck's a nark, an' swears some more,
An' then: "Wot is the strength uv this 'ere war?"

I tells 'im wot I read about the 'Uns,
    An' wot they done in Beljum an' in France,
Wiv drivin' Janes an' kids before their guns,
    An' never givin' blokes a stray dawg's chance;
An' 'ow they think they've got the whole world beat.
Sez 'e, "I'll crack the first Dutch cow I meet!"

Mick listens, while I tells 'im 'ow they starts
    Be burnin' pore coves 'omes an' killin' kids,
An' comin' it reel crook wiv decent tarts,
    An' fightin' foul, as orl the rules forbids,
Leavin' a string uv stiff-uns in their track.
Sez Mick, "The dirty cows! They *wants* a crack!"

'E chews it over solid fer a bit,
    Workin' 'is copper-top a double shift.
I don't need specs to see that 'e wus 'it
    Be somethin' more than Rosie's little rift.
"If they'd done that," 'e sez, "out 'ere—Ar, rats!
Why don't ole England belt 'em in the slats?"

Then Mick gits up an' starts another fag.
    "Ar, well," 'e sez, "it's no affair uv mine,
If I don't work they'd pinch me on the vag;
    But I'm not keen to fight so toffs kin dine
On pickled olives … *Blarst* the flamin' war!
I ain't got nothin' worth the fightin' for.

"So long," 'e sez. "I got ter trade me stock;
    An' when yeh 'ear I've took a soljer's job

I give yeh leave to say I've done me block
    An' got a flock uv weevils in me knob."
An' then, orf-'anded-like, 'e arsts me: "Say,
Wot are they slingin' soljers fer their pay?"

I tells 'im; an' 'e sez to me, "So long.
    Some day this rabbit trade will git me beat."
An' Ginger Mick shoves thro' the markit throng,
    An' gits 'is barrer out into the street.
An', as 'e goes, I 'ears 'is gentle roar:
"Rabbee! Wile Rabbee! … Blarst the flamin' war!"

THE CALL OF STOUSH

WOT price ole Ginger Mick? 'E's done a break—
 Gone to the flamin' war to stoush the foe.
Wus it fer glory, or a woman's sake?
 Ar, arst me somethin' easy! I dunno.
'Is Kharki clobber set 'im off a treat,
That's all I know; 'is motive's got me beat.

Ole Mick e's trainin' up in Cairo now;
 An' all the cops in Spadger's Lane is sad.
They miss 'is music in the midnight row
 Wot time the pushes mix it good an' glad.
Fer 'e wus one o' them, you understand,
Wot "soils the soshul life uv this fair land."

A peb wus Mick; a leery bloke wus 'e,
 Low down, an' given to the brimmin' cup;
The sort o' chap that coves like you an' me,
 Don't mix wiv, 'cos of our strick bringin's-up.
An' 'e wus sich becos unseein' Fate
Lobbed 'im in life a 'undred years too late.

'E wus a man uv vierlence, wus Mick,
 Coarse wiv 'is speech an' in 'is manner low,
Slick wiv 'is 'ands, an' 'andy wiv a brick
 When bricks wus needful to defeat a foe.

An' now 'e's gone an' mizzled to the war,
An' some blokes 'as the nerve to arst "Wot for?"

Wot for? Gawstruth! 'E wus no patriot
    That sits an' brays advice in days uv strife;
'E never flapped no flags nor sich like rot;
    'E never sung "Gawsave" in all 'is life.
'E wus dispised be them that make sich noise;
But now—O strike!—'e's "one uv our brave boys."

'E's one uv our brave boys, all right, all right.
    'Is early trainin' down in Spadger's Lane
Done 'im no 'arm fer this 'ere orl-in fight;
    'Is loss o' culcher is 'is country's gain.
'Im wiv 'is carst-ir'n chiv an' leery ways—
An' swell tarts 'eavin' 'im sweet words o' praise.

Why did 'e go? 'E 'ad a decent job,
    'Is tart an' 'im they could 'a' made it right.
Why does a wild bull fight to guard the mob?
    Why does a bloomin' bull-ant look fer fight?
Why does a rooster scrap an' flap an' crow?
'E went becos 'e dam well 'ad to go.

'E never spouted no 'igh-soundin' stuff
    About stern jooty an' 'is country's call;
But, in 'is way, 'e 'eard it right enough
    A-callin' like the shout uv "On the Ball!"
Wot time the footer brings the clicks great joy,
An' Saints er Carlton roughs it up wiv 'Roy.

The call wot came to cave-men in the days
    When rocks wus stylish in the scrappin' line;
The call wot knights 'eard in the minstrel's lays,

That sent 'em in tin soots to Palerstine;
The call wot draws all fighters to the fray
It come to Mick, an' Mick 'e must obey.

The Call uv Stoush! ... It's older than the 'ills.
    Lovin' an' fightin'—there's no more to tell
Concernin' men. An' when that feelin' thrills
    The blood uv them 'oo's fathers mixed it well,
They 'ave to 'eed it—bein' 'ow they're built—
As traders 'ave to 'eed the clink uv gilt.

An' them whose gilt 'as stuffed 'em stiff wiv pride
    An' 'aughty scorn uv blokes like Ginger Mick—
I sez to them, put sich crook thorts aside,
    An' don't lay on the patronage too thick.
Orl men is brothers when it comes to lash
An' 'aughty scorn an' Culcher does their dash.

War ain't no giddy garden feete—it's war:
    A game that calls up love an' 'atred both.
An' them that shudders at the sight o' gore,
    An' shrinks to 'ear a drunken soljer's oath,
Must 'ide be'ind the man wot 'eaves the bricks,
An' thank their Gawd for all their Ginger Micks.

Becos 'e never 'ad the chance to find
    The glory o' the world by land an' sea,
Becos the beauty 'idin' in 'is mind
    Was not writ plain fer blokes like you an' me,
They calls 'im crook; but in 'im I 'ave found
Wot makes a man a man the world around.

Be'ind that dile uv 'is, as 'ard as sin,
    Wus strange, soft thorts that never yet showed out;

An' down in Spadger's Lane, in dirt an' din,
    'E dreamed sich dreams as poits sing about.
'E's 'ad 'is visions uv the Bonzer Tart;
An' stoushed some coot to ease 'is swellin' 'eart.

Lovin' an' fightin' … when the tale is told,
    That's all there is to it; an' in their way
Them brave an' noble 'ero blokes uv old
    Wus Ginger Micks—the crook 'uns uv their day.
Jist let the Call uv Stoush give 'im 'is chance
An' Ginger Mick's the 'ero of Romance.

So Ginger Mick 'e's mizzled to the war;
    Joy in 'is 'eart, an' wild dreams in 'is brain;
Gawd 'elp the foe that 'e goes gunnin' for
    If tales is true they tell in Spadger's Lane—
Tales that ud fairly freeze the gentle 'earts
Uv them 'oo knits 'is socks—the Culchered Tarts.

THE PUSH

BECOS a crook done in a prince, an' narked an Emperor,
　　An' struck a light that set the world aflame;
Becos the bugles East an' West sooled on the dawgs o' war,
　　A bloke called Ginger Mick 'as found 'is game—
Found 'is game an' found 'is brothers, 'oo wus strangers in 'is sight,
Till they shed their silly clobber an' put on the duds fer fight.

Yes, they've shed their silly clobber an' the other stuff they wore
　　Fer to 'ide the man beneath it in the past;
An' each man is the clean, straight man 'is Maker meant 'im for,
　　An' each man knows 'is brother man at last.
Shy strangers, till a bugle blast preached 'oly brother'ood;
But mateship they 'ave found at last; an' they 'ave found it good.

So the lumper, an' the lawyer, an' the chap 'oo shifted sand,
　　They are cobbers wiv the cove 'oo drove a quill;
The knut 'oo swung a cane upon the Block, 'e takes the 'and
　　Uv the coot 'oo swung a pick on Broken 'Ill;
An' Privit Clord Augustus drills wiv Privit Snarky Jim—
They are both Australian soljers, w'ich is good enough fer 'im.

It's good enough fer orl uv 'em, as orl uv 'em 'ave seen
　　Since they got the same glad clobber next their skins;
An' the bloke 'oo 'olds the boodle an' the coot wivout a bean,
　　Why, they knock around like little Kharki twins.

An' they got a common lingo, w'ich is growin' mighty thick
Wiv ixpressive contributions frum the stock uv Ginger Mick.

'E 'as struck it fer a moral. Ginger's found 'is game at last,
    An' 'e's took to it like ducklin's take to drink;
An' 'is slouchin' an' 'is grouchin' an' 'is loafin' uv the past—
    'E's done wiv 'em, an' dumped 'em down the sink.
'E's a bright an' shinin' sample uv a the'ry that I 'old:
That ev'ry 'eart that ever pumped is good fer chunks o' gold.

Ev'ry feller is a gold mine if yeh take an' work 'im right:
    It is shinin' on the surface now an' then;
An' there's some is easy sinkin', but there's some wants dynermite,
    Fer they looks a 'opeless prospect—yet they're men.
An' Ginger—'ard-shell Ginger's showin' signs that 'e will pay;
But it took a flamin' world-war fer to blarst 'is crust away.

But they took 'im an' they drilled 'im an' they shipped 'im overseas
    Wiv a crowd uv blokes 'e never met before.
'E rowed wiv 'em, an' scrapped wiv 'em, an' done some tall C.B.'s,
    An' 'e lobbed wiv 'em on Egyp's sandy shore.
Then Pride o' Race lay 'olt on 'im, an' Mick shoves out 'is chest
To find 'imself Australian an' blood brothers wiv the rest.

So I gits some reel good readin' in the letter wot 'e sent—
    Tho' the spellin's pretty rotten now an' then.
"I 'ad the joes at first," 'e sez; "but now I'm glad I went,
    Fer it's shine to be among reel, livin' men.
An' it's grand to be Australian, an' to say, it good an' loud
When yeh bump a forrin country wiv sich fellers as our crowd.

" 'Struth! I've 'ung around me native land fer close on thirty year,
    An' I never knoo wot men me cobbers were:
Never knoo that toffs wus white men till I met 'em over 'ere—

Blokes an' coves I sort o' snouted over there.
Yes, I loafed aroun' me country; an' I never knoo 'er then;
But the reel, ribuck Australia's 'ere, among the fightin' men.

"We've slung the swank fer good an' all; it don't fit in our plan;
    To skite uv birth an' boodle is a crime.
A man wiv us, why, 'e's a man becos 'e is a man,
    An' a reel red-'ot Australian ev'ry time.
Fer dawg an' side an' snobbery is down an' out fer keeps.
It's grit an' reel good fellership that gits yeh friends in 'eaps.

"There's a bloke 'oo shipped when I did; 'e wus lately frum 'is ma,
    'Oo 'ad filled 'im full uv notions uv 'is birth;
An' 'e overworked 'is aitches till 'e got the loud 'Ha-ha'
    Frum the fellers, but 'e wouldn't come to earth.
I bumped 'is lordship, name o' Keith, an' 'ad a little row,
An' 'e lost some chunks uv beauty; but 'e's good Australian now.

"There is Privit Snifty Thompson, 'oo wus once a Sydney rat,
    An' 'e 'ung around the Rocks when 'e wus young.
There's little Smith uv Collin'wood, wiv fags stuck in 'is 'at,
    An' a string uv dirty insults on 'is tongue.
A corperil took them in 'and—a lad frum Lameroo.
Now both is nearly gentlemen, an' good Australians too.

"There's one, 'e doesn't tork a lot, 'e sez 'is name is Trent,
    Jist a privit, but 'e knows 'is drill a treat;
A stand-orf bloke, but reel good pals wiv fellers in 'is tent;
    But 'is 'ome an' 'istoree 'as got 'em beat.
They reckon when 'e starts to bleed 'e'll stain 'is Kharki blue;
An' 'is lingo smells uv Oxford—but 'e's good Australian too.

"Then there's Lofty Craig uv Queensland, 'oo's a special pal uv mine;
    Slow an' shy, an' kind o' nervous uv 'is height;

An' Jupp, 'oo owns a copper show, an' arsts us out to dine
    When we're doo fer leave in Cairo uv a night.
An' there's Bills an' Jims an' Bennos, an' there's Roys an' 'Arolds too,
An' they're cobbers, an' they're brothers, an' Australians thro' an' thro'.

"There is farmers frum the Mallee, there is bushmen down frum Bourke,
    There's college men wiv letters to their name;
There is grafters, an' there's blokes 'oo never done a 'ard day's work
    Till they tumbled, wiv the rest, into the game—
An' they're drillin' 'ere together, men uv ev'ry creed an' kind.
It's Australia! Solid! Dinkum! that 'as left the land be'ind.

"An' if yeh want a slushy, or a station overseer,
    Or a tinker, or a tailor, or a snob,
Or a 'andy bloke wiv 'orses, or a minin' ingineer,
    Why, we've got the very man to do yer job.
Butcher, baker, undertaker, or a Caf' de Pary chef,
'E is waitin', keen an' ready, in the little A.I.F.

"An' they've drilled us. Strike me lucky! but they've drilled us fer a cert!
    We 'ave trod around ole Egyp's burnin' sand
Till I tells meself at evenin', when I'm wringin' out me shirt,
    That we're built uv wire an' green-'ide in our land.
Strike! I thort I knoo 'ard yakker, w'ich I've tackled many ways,
But uv late I've took a tumble I bin dozin' orl me days.

"It's a game, lad," writes ole Ginger. "It's a game I'm likin' grand.
    An' I'm tryin' fer a stripe to fill in time.
I 'ave took a pull on shicker fer the honour uv me land,
    An' I'm umpty round the chest an' feelin' prime.
Yeh kin tell Rose, if yeh see 'er, I serloots 'er o'er the foam,
An' we'll 'ave a cray fer supper when I comes a-marchin' 'ome."

So ole Ginger sends a letter, an' 'is letter's good to read,
  Fer the things 'e sez, an' some things 'e leaves out;
An' when a bloke like 'im wakes up an' starts to take a 'eed,
  Well, it's sort o' worth the writin' 'ome about.
'E's one uv many little things Australia chanced to find
She never knoo she 'ad around till bugles cleared 'er mind.

Becos ole Europe lost 'er block an' started 'eavin' bricks,
  Becos the bugles wailed a song uv war,
We found reel gold down in the 'earts uv orl our Ginger Micks
  We never thort worth minin' fer before.
An' so, I'm tippin' we will pray, before our win is scored:
"Thank God fer Mick, an' Bill an' Jim, an' little brother Clord."

SARI BAIR

SO, they've struck their streak o' trouble, an' they got it in the neck,
An' there's more than one ole pal o' mine 'as 'anded in 'is check;
But Ginger still takes nourishment; 'e's well, but breathin' 'ard.
An' so 'e sends the strength uv it scrawled on a chunk uv card.

"On the day we 'it the transport there wus cheerin' on the pier,
An' the girls wus wavin' hankies as they dropped a partin' tear,
An' we felt like little 'eroes as we watched the crowd recede,
Fer we sailed to prove Australia, an' our boastin' uv the breed.

"There wus Trent, ex-toff, uv England; there wus Green, ex-pug, uv 'Loo;
There wus me, an' Craig uv Queensland, wiv 'is 'ulkin' six-foot-two;
An' little Smith uv Collin'wood, 'oo 'owled a rag-time air,
On the day we left the Leeuwin, bound nor'-west for Gawd-knows-where.

"On the day we come to Cairo wiv its niggers an' its din,
To fill our eyes wiv desert sand, our souls wiv Eastern sin,
There wus cursin' an' complainin'; we wus 'ungerin' fer fight—
Little imertation soljers full uv vanity an' skite.

"Then they worked us—Gawd! they worked us, till we knoo wot drillin'
        meant;
Till men begun to feel like men, an' wasters to repent,
Till we grew to 'ate all Egyp', an' its desert, an' its stinks:
On the days we drilled at Mena in the shadder uv the Sphinx.

"Then Green uv Sydney swore an oath they meant to 'old us tight,
A crowd uv flamin' ornaments wivout a chance to fight;
But little Smith uv Collin'wood, he whistled 'im a toon,
An' sez, 'Aw, take a pull, lad; there'll be whips o' stoushin' soon.'

"Then the waitin', weary waitin', while we itched to meet the foe!
But we'd done wiv fancy skitin' an' the comic op'ra show.
We wus soljers—finished soljers, an' we felt it in our veins
On the day we trod the desert on ole Egyp's sandy plains.

"An' Trent 'e said it wus a bore, an' all uv us wus blue,
An' Craig, the giant, never joked the way 'e used to do.
But little Smith uv Collin'wood 'e 'ummed a little song,
An' said, 'You leave it to the 'eads. O now we sha'n't be long!'

"Then Sari Bair, O Sari Bair, 'twus you wot seen it done,
The day the transports rode yer bay beneath a smilin' sun.
We boasted much, an' toasted much; but where yer tide line creeps,
'Twus you, me dainty Sari Bair, that seen us play fer keeps.

"We wus full uv savage skitin' while they kep' us on the shelf—
(Now I tell yeh, square an' 'onest, I wus doubtin' us meself);
But we proved it, good an' plenty, that our lads can do an' dare,
On the day we walloped Abdul o'er the sands o' Sari Bair.

"Luck wus out wiv Green uv Sydney, where 'e stood at my right 'and,
Fer they plunked 'im on the transport 'fore 'e got a chance to land.
Then I saw 'em kill a feller wot I knoo in Camberwell,
Somethin' sort o' went inside me—an' the rest wus bloody 'ell.

"Thro' the smoke I seen 'im strivin', Craig uv Queensland, tall an' strong,
Like an 'arvester at 'ay-time singin', swingin' to the song.
An' little Smith uv Collin'wood, 'e 'owled a fightin' tune,
On the day we chased Mahomet over Sari's sandy dune.

"An' Sari Bair, O Sari Bair, you seen 'ow it wus done,
The transports dancin' in yer bay beneath the bonzer sun;
An' speckled o'er yer gleamin' shore the little 'uddled 'eaps
That showed at last the Southern breed could play the game fer keeps.

"We found 'im, Craig uv Queensland, stark, 'is 'and still on' is gun.
We found too many more besides, when that fierce scrap wus done.
An' little Smith uv Collin'wood, he crooned a mournful air,
The night we planted 'em beneath the sands uv Sari Bair.

"On the day we took the transport there wus cheerin' on the pier,
An' we wus little chiner gawds; an' now we're sittin' 'ere,
Wiv the taste uv blood an' battle on the lips uv ev'ry man
An' ev'ry man jist 'opin' fer to end as we began.

"Fer Green is gone, an' Craig is gone, an' Gawd! 'ow many more!
Who sleep the sleep at Sari Bair beside that sunny shore!
An' little Smith uv Collin'wood, a bandage 'round 'is 'ead,
He 'ums a savage song an' vows quick vengeance fer the dead.

"But Sari Bair, me Sari Bair, the secrets that you 'old
Will shake the 'earts uv Southern men when all the tale is told;
An' when they git the strength uv it, there'll never be the need
To call too loud fer fightin' men among the Southern breed."

GINGER'S COBBER

"'E WEARS perjarmer soots an' cleans 'is teeth,"
  That's wot I reads. It fairly knocked me flat,
"Me soljer cobber, be the name o' Keith."
  Well, if that ain't the limit, strike me fat!
The sort that Ginger Mick would think beneath
'Is notice once. Perjarmers! Cleans 'is teeth!

Ole Ginger Mick 'as sent a billy-doo
  Frum somew'ere on the earth where fightin's thick.
The Censor wus a sport to let it thro',
  Considerin' the choice remarks o' Mick.
It wus that 'ot, I'm wond'rin' since it came
It didn't set the bloomin' mail aflame.

I'd love to let yeh 'ave it word fer word;
  But, strickly, it's a bit above the odds;
An' there's remarks that's 'ardly ever 'eard
  Amongst the company to w'ich we nods.
It seems they use the style in Ginger's trench
Wot's written out an' 'anded to the Bench.

I tones the langwidge down to soot the ears
  Of sich as me an' you resorts wiv now.
If I should give it jist as it appears
  Pertic'lar folk might want ter make a row.

But say, yeh'd think ole Ginger wus a pote
If yeh could read some juicy bits 'e's wrote.

It's this noo pal uv 'is that tickles me;
    'E's got a mumma, an' 'is name is Keith.
A knut upon the Block 'e used to be,
    'Ome 'ere; the sort that flashes golden teeth,
An' wears 'ot socks, an' torks a lot o' guff;
But Ginger sez they're cobbers till they snuff.

It come about like this: Mick spragged 'im first
    Fer swankin' it too much aboard the ship.
'E 'ad nice manners an' 'e never cursed;
    Which set Mick's teeth on edge, as you may tip.
Likewise, 'e 'ad two silver brushes, w'ich
'Is mumma give 'im, 'cos 'e fancied sich.

Mick pinched 'em. Not, as you will understand,
    Becos uv any base desire fer loot,
But jist becos, in that rough soljer band,
    Them silver-backed arrangements didn't soot;
An' etiket must be observed always.
(They fetched ten drinks in Cairo, Ginger says.)

That satisfied Mick's honour fer a bit,
    But still 'e picks at Keith fer exercise,
An' all the other blokes near 'as a fit
    To see Mick squirm at Keith's perlite replies,
Till one day Keith 'owls back "You flamin' cow!"
Then Mick permotes 'im, an' they 'as a row.

I sez "permotes 'im," fer, yeh'll understand,
    Ole Ginger 'as 'is pride o' class orl right;
'E's not the bloke to go an' soil 'is 'and

Be stoushin' any coot that wants to fight.
'Im, that 'as 'ad 'is chances more'n once
Up at the Stajum, ain't no bloomin' dunce.

Yeh'll 'ave to guess wot sort o' fight took place.
    Keith learnt 'is boxin' at a "culcher" school.
The first three rounds, to save 'im frum disgrace,
    Mick kids 'im on an' plays the gentle fool.
An' then 'e outs 'im wiv a little tap,
An' tells 'im, 'e's a reg'lar plucky chap.

They likes each other better after that,
    Fer Ginger alwiz 'ad a reel soft spot
Fer blokes 'oo 'ad some man beneath their 'at,
    An' never whined about the jolts they got.
Still, pride o' class kept 'em frum gettin' thick.
It's 'ard to git right next to Ginger Mick.

Then comes Gallipoli an' wot Mick calls
    "An orl-in push fight multerplied be ten;"
An' one be one the orfficers they falls,
    Until there's no one left to lead the men.
Fer 'arf a mo' they 'esitates stock still;
Fer 'oo's to lead 'em up the flamin' 'ill?

'Oo is to lead 'em if it ain't the bloke
    'Oo's 'eaded pushes down in Spadger's Lane,
Since 'e first learnt to walk an' swear an' smoke,
    An' mixed it willin' both fer fun an' gain—
That narsty, ugly, vi'lent man, 'oo's got
Grip on the minds uv men when blood runs 'ot?

Mick led 'em; an' be'ind 'im up the rise,
    'Owlin' an' cursin', comes that mumma's boy,

'Is cobber, Keith, with that look in 'is eyes
    To give the 'eart uv any leader joy.
An' langwidge! If 'is mar at 'ome 'ad 'eard
She would 'a' threw a fit at ev'ry word.

Mick dunno much about wot 'appened then,
    Excep' 'e felt 'is Dream uv Stoush come true;
Fer 'im an' Keith they fought like fifty men,
    An' felt like gawds wiv ev'ry breath they drew,
Then Ginger gits it solid in the neck,
An' flops; an' counts on passin' in 'is check.

When 'e come to, the light wus gettin' dim,
    The ground wus cold an' sodden underneath,
Someone is lyin' right 'longside uv 'im.
    Groanin' wiv pain, 'e turns, an' sees it's Keith—
Keith, wiv 'is rifle cocked, an' starin' 'ard
Ahead. An' now 'e sez "'Ow is it, pard?"

Mick gently lifts 'is 'ead an' looks around.
    There ain't another flamin' soul in sight,
They're covered be a bit o' risin' ground,
    An' rifle-fire is cracklin' to the right.
"Down!" sez the mumma's joy. "Don't show yer 'ead!
Unless yeh want it loaded full o' lead."

Then, bit be bit, Mick gits the strength uv it.
    They wus so occupied wiv privit scraps,
They never noticed 'ow they come to git
    Right out ahead uv orl the other chaps.
They've bin cut orf, wiv jist one little chance
Uv gittin' back. Mick seen it at a glance.

"'Ere, Kid," 'e sez, "you sneak around that 'ill.
  I'm down an' out; an' you kin tell the boys;"
Keith don't reply to 'im but jist lies still,
  An' signs to Ginger not to make a noise.
"'Ere, you!" sez Mick, "I ain't the man to funk—
I won't feel 'ome-sick. Imshee! Do a bunk!"

Keith bites 'is lips; 'e never turns 'is 'ead.
  "Wot in the 'ell;" sez Mick, "'ere, wot's yer game?"
"I'm an Australian," that wus all 'e said,
  An' pride took 'old o' Mick to 'ear that name—
A noo, glad pride that ain't the pride o' class—
An' Mick's contempt, it took the count at lars'!

All night they stayed there, Mick near mad wiv pain,
  An' Keith jist lettin' up 'is watchful eye
To ease Mick's wounds an' bind 'em up again,
  An' give 'im water, w'ile 'imself went dry.
Brothers they wus, 'oo found their brother'ood
That night on Sari Bair, an' found it good.

Brothers they wus. I'm wond'rin', as I read
  This scrawl uv Mick's, an' git its meanin' plain,
If you, 'oo never give these things no 'eed,
  Ain't got some brothers down in Spadger's Lane—
Brothers you never 'ad the chance to meet
Becos they got no time fer Collins Street.

"I'm an Australian." Well, it takes the bun!
  It's got that soft spot in the 'eart o' Mick.
But don't make no mistake; 'e don't gush none,
  Or come them "brother'ood" remarks too thick.
'E only writes, *This Keith's a decent coot,*
Cobber o' mine, an' white from cap to boot.

"'*E wears perjarmers an' 'e cleans 'is teeth,*"
   The sort o' bloke that Ginger once dispised!
But once a man shows metal underneath,
   Cobbers is found, an' brothers reckernised.
Fer, when a bloke's soul-clobber's shed in war,
'E looks the sort o' man Gawd meant 'im for.

THE SINGING SOLDIERS

WHEN I'm sittin' in me dug-out wiv me rifle on me knees,
An' a yowlin', 'owlin' chorus comes a-floatin' up the breeze—
    Jist a bit o' 'Bonnie Mary' or 'Long Way to Tipperary'—
Then I know I'm in Australia, took an' planted overseas.
      They've bin up agin it solid since we crossed the flamin' foam;
      But they're singin'—alwiz singin'—since we left the wharf at 'ome.

"O, its 'On the Mississippi' or 'Me Grey 'Ome in the West.'
If it's death an' 'ell nex' minute they must git it orf their chest.
      'Ere's a snatch o' 'When yer Roamin'—When yer Roamin' in the
          Gloamin'.'
'Struth! The first time that I 'eard it, wiv me 'ead on Rosie's breast,
      We wus comin' frum a picnic in a Ferntree Gully train …
      But the shrapnel made the music when I 'eard it sung again."

So I gits it straight frum Ginger in 'is letter 'ome to me,
On a dirty scrap o' paper wiv the writin' 'ard to see.
      "Strike!" sez 'e. "It sounds like skitin'; but they're singin' while they're
fightin';
An' they socks it into Abdul to the toon o' 'Nancy Lee.'
      An' I seen a bloke this mornin' wiv 'is arm blown to a rag,
      'Ummin' 'Break the Noos to Mother,' w'ile 'e sucked a soothin' fag.

"Now, the British Tommy curses, an' the French does fancy stunts,
An' the Turk 'e 'owls to Aller, an' the Gurkha grins an' grunts;
      But our boys is singin', singin', while the blinded shells is flingin'

Mud an' death inter the trenches in them 'eavens called the Fronts.
    An' I guess their souls keep singin' when they gits the tip to go … "
    So I gits it, straight frum Ginger; an' Gawstruth! 'e ort to know.

An' 'is letter gits me thinkin' when I read sich tales as these,
An' I takes a look around me at the paddicks an' the trees;
    When I 'ears the thrushes trillin', when I 'ear the magpies fillin'
All the air frum earth to 'eaven wiv their careless melerdies—
    It's the sunshine uv the country, caught an' turned to bonzer notes;
    It's the sunbeams changed to music pourin' frum a thousand throats.

Can a soljer 'elp 'is singin' when 'e's born in sich a land?
Wiv the sunshine an' the music pourin' out on ev'ry 'and,
    Where the very air is singin', an' each breeze that blows is bringin'
'Armony an' mirth an' music fit to beat the blazin' band.
    On the march, an' in the trenches, when a swingin' chorus starts,
    They are pourin' bottled sunshine of their 'Omeland frum their 'earts.

O I've 'eard it, Lord, I've 'eard it since the days when I wus young,
On the beach an' in the bar-room, in the bush I've 'eard it sung;
    "Belle Mahone" an' "Annie Laurie," "Sweet Marie" to "Tobermory,"
Common toons and common voices, but I've 'eard 'em when they rung
    Wiv full, 'appy 'earts be'ind 'em, careless as a thrush's song—
    Wiv me arm around me cliner, an' me notions fur from wrong.

So they growed wiv 'earts a-singin' since the days uv careless kids;
Beefin' out an 'appy chorus jist when Mother Nacher bids;
    Singin', wiv their notes a-quiver, "Down upon the Swanee River,"
Them's sich times I'd not be sellin' fer a stack uv golden quids.
    An' they're singin', still they're singin', to the sound uv guns an' drums,
    As they sung one golden Springtime underneath the wavin' gums.

When they socked it to the *Southland* wiv our sunny boys aboard—
Them that stopped a dam torpeder, an' a knock-out punch wus scored;

Tho' their 'ope o' life grew murky, wiv the ship 'ead over turkey,
Dread o' death an' fear o' drownin' wus jist trifles they ignored.
    They spat out the blarsted ocean, an' they filled 'emselves wiv air,
    An' they passed along the chorus of "Australia will be There."

Yes, they sung it in the water; an' a bloke aboard a ship
Sez 'e *knoo* they wus Australians be the way they give it lip—
    Sung it to the soothin' motion of the dam devourin' ocean
Like a crowd o' seaside trippers in to 'ave a little dip.
    When I 'eard that tale, I tell yeh, straight, I sort o' felt a choke;
    Fer I seemed to 'ear 'em singin', an' I know that sort o' bloke,

Yes, I know 'im; so I seen 'im, barrackin' Eternity.
An' the land that 'e wus born in is the land that mothered me.
    Strike! I ain't no sniv'lin' blighter; but I own me eyes git brighter
When I see 'em pokin' mullock at the everlastin' sea:
    When I 'ear 'em mockin' terror wiv a merry slab o' mirth,
    'Ell! I'm proud I bin to *gaol* in sich a land as give 'em birth!

                    *   *   *

"When I'm sittin' in me dug-out wiv the bullets droppin' near,"
Writes ole Ginger; "an' a chorus smacks me in the flamin' ear:
    P'raps a song that Rickards billed, er p'raps a line o' 'Waltz Matilder',
Then I feel I'm in Australia, took an' shifted over 'ere.
    Till the music sort o' gits me, an' I lets me top notes roam
    While I treats the gentle foeman to a chunk uv ' 'Ome, Sweet 'Ome.' "

They wus singin' on the troopship, they wus singin' in the train;
When they left their land be'ind 'em they wus shoutin' a refrain,
    An' I'll bet they 'ave a chorus, gay an' glad in greetin' for us,
When their bit uv scrappin's over, an' they lob back 'ome again …
    An' the blokes that ain't returnin'—blokes that's paid the biggest price,
    They go singin', singin', singin' to the Gates uv Paradise.

IN SPADGER'S LANE

OLE Mother Moon 'oo yanks 'er beamin' dile
    Acrost the sky when we've grown sick o' day,
She's like some fat ole Jane 'oo loves to smile
    On all concerned, an' smooth our faults away;
An', like a woman, tries to 'ide again
The sores an' scars crool day 'as made too plain.

To all the earth she gives the soft glad-eye;
    She picks no fav'rits in this world o' men;
She peeps in nooks, where 'appy lovers sigh,
    To make their joy more bonzer still; an' then,
O'er Spadger's Lane she waves a podgy 'and,
An' turns the scowlin' slums to Fairyland.

Aw, strike! I'm gettin' soft in my ole age!
    I'm growin' mushy wiv the passin' years.
Me! that 'as called it weakness to ingage
    In sloppy thorts that coax the pearly tears.
But say, me state o' mind I can't ixplain
When I seen Rose lars' night in Spadger's Lane.

'Twas Spadger's Lane where Ginger Mick 'ung out
    Before 'e took to follerin' the Flag;
The Lane that echoed to 'is drunken shout
    When 'e lobbed 'omeward on a gaudy jag.

Now Spadger's Lane knows Ginger Mick no more,
Fer 'e's become an 'ero at the War.

A flamin' 'ero at the War, that's Mick.
    An' Rose—'is Rose, is waitin' in the Lane,
Nursin' 'er achin' 'eart, an' lookin' sick
    As she crawls out to work an' 'ome again,
Givin' the bird to blokes 'oo'd be 'er "friend,"
An' prayin', wiv the rest, fer wars to end.

Quite right; I'm growin' sloppy fer a cert;
    But I must git it orf me chest or bust.
So 'ere's a song about a grievin' skirt.
    An' love, an' Ginger Mick, an' maiden trust!
The choky sort o' song that fetches tears
When blokes is full o' sentiment—or beers.

Lars' night, when I sneaks down to taste again
    The sights an' sounds I used to know so well,
The moon wus shinin' over Spadger's Lane,
    Sof'nin' the sorrer where 'er kind light fell;
Sof'nin' an' soothin', like it wus 'er plan
To make ixcuses fer the sins uv man.

Frum shadder inter shadder, up the street,
    A prowlin' moll sneaks by, wiv eyes all 'ate,
Dodgin' some unseen John, 'oo's sure, slow feet
    Comes tappin' after, certin as 'er fate;
In some back crib, a shicker's loud 'owled verse
Stops sudden, wiv a crash, an' then a curse.

Low down, a splotch o' red, where 'angs a blind
    Before the winder of a Chow caboose,
Shines in the dead black wall, an' frum be'ind,

Like all the cats o' Chinertown broke loose,
A mad Chow fiddle wails a two-note toon …
An' then I seen 'er, underneath the moon.

Rosie the Rip they calls 'er in the Lane;
    Fer she wus alwiz willin' wiv 'er 'an's,
An' uses 'em to make 'er meanin' plain
    In ways that Spadger's beauties understan's.
But when ole Ginger played to snare 'er 'eart,
Rosie the Rip wus jist the soft, weak tart.

'Igh in 'er winder she wus leanin' out,
    Swappin' remarks wiv fat ole Mother Moon.
The things around I clean fergot about—
    Fergot the fiddle an' its crook Chow toon;
I only seen one woman in the light
Achin' to learn 'er forchin frum the night.

Ole Ginger's Rose! To see 'er sittin' there,
    The moonlight shinin' fair into 'er face,
An' sort o' touchin' gentle on 'er 'air,
    It made me fair fergit the time an' place.
I feels I'm peepin' where I never ought,
An' tries 'arf not to 'ear the words I caught.

One soljer's sweet'eart, that wus wot I seen:
    One out o' thousands grievin' thro' the land.
A tart frum Spadger's or a weepin' queen—
    Wot's there between 'em, when yeh understand?
She 'olds fer Mick, wiv all 'is ugly chiv,
The best a lovin' woman 'as to give.

The best a woman 'as to give—Aw, 'Struth!
    When war, an' grief, an' trouble's on the land

Sometimes a bloke gits glimpses uv the truth
    An' sweats 'is soul to try an' understand …
An' then the World, like some offishus John,
Shoves out a beefy 'and, an' moves 'im on.

So I seen Rose; an' so, on that same night
    I seen a million women grievin' there.
Ole Mother Moon she showed to me a sight
    She sees around the World, most everyw'ere.
Sneakin' beneath the shadder uv the wall
I seen, an' learned, an' understood it all.

An' as I looks at Rosie, dreamin' there,
    'Er 'ead drops on 'er arms … I seems to wake;
I sees the moonlight streamin' on 'er 'air;
    I 'ears 'er sobbin' like 'er 'eart ud break.
An' me there, pryin' on 'er misery.
"Gawstruth!" I sez, "This ain't no place fer me!"

On my tip-toes I sneaks the way I came—
    (The crook Chow fiddle ain't done yowlin' yet)—
An' tho' I tells it to me bitter shame—
    I'm gittin' soft as 'ell—me eyes wus wet.
An' that stern John, as I go moochin' by
Serloots me wiv a cold, unfeelin' eye.

The fat ole Mother Moon she's got a 'eart.
    An' so I like to think, when she looks down
Wiv 'er soft gaze upon some weepin' tart
    In bonzer gardens or the slums o' town;
She soothes 'em, mother-like, wiv podgy 'ands,
An' makes 'em dream agen uv peaceful lands.

THE STRAIGHT GRIFFIN

" 'EROES? Orright. You 'ave it 'ow yeh like.
    Throw up yer little 'at an' come the glad;
But not too much 'Three-'Earty-Cheers' fer Mike;
    There's other things that 'e'll be wantin' bad.
The boys won't 'ave them kid-stakes on their mind
Wivout there's somethin' solider be'ind."

Now that's the dinkum oil frum Ginger Mick,
    In 'orspital, somew'ere be'ind the front;
Plugged in the neck, an' lately pretty sick,
    But now right on the converlescent stunt.
"I'm on the mend," 'e writes, "an' nearly doo
To come the 'ero act agen—Scene two."

I'd sent some papers, knowin' 'ow time drags
    Wiv blokes in blankits, waitin' fer a cure.
"An' 'Struth!" Mick writes, "the way they et them rags
    Yeh'd think that they'd bin weaned on litrachure.
They wrestled thro' frum 'Births' to 'Lost and Found';
They even give the Leaders 'arf a round."

Mick spent a bonzer day propped up in bed,
    Soothin' 'is soul wiv ev'ry sportin' page;
But in the football noos the things 'e read
    Near sent 'im orf 'is top wiv 'oly rage;

The way 'is team 'as mucked it earned 'is curse;
But 'e jist swallered it—becos uv nurse.

An' then this 'eadline 'it 'im wiv bokays;
    "*Australian Heroes!*" is the song it makes.
Mick reads the boys them ringin' words o' praise;
    But they jist grins a bit an' sez "Kid stakes!"
Sez Mick to nurse, "You tumble wot I am?
A bloomin' little 'ero. Pass the jam!"

Mick don't say much uv nurse; but 'tween the lines—
    ('Im bein' not too strong on gushin' speech)—
I seem to see some tell-tale sort o' signs.
    Sez 'e, "Me nurse-girl is a bonzer peach."
An' then 'e 'as a line: " 'Er sad, sweet look."
'Struth! Ginger must 'a' got it frum a book.

Say, I can see ole Ginger, plain as plain,
    Purrin' to feel the touch uv 'er cool 'and,
Grinnin' a bit to kid 'is wound don't pain,
    An' yappin' tork she don't 'arf understand,
That makes 'er wonder if, back where she lives,
They're all reel men be'ind them ugly chivs.

But that's orright. Ole Ginger ain't no flirt.
    "You tell my Rose," 'e writes, "she's still the sweet.
An' if Long Jim gits messin' round that skirt,
    When I come back I'll do 'im up a treat.
Tell 'im, if all me arms an' legs is lame
I'll *bite* the blighter if 'e comes that game!"

There's jealousy! But Ginger needn't fret.
    Rose is fer 'im, an' Jim ain't on 'er card;
An' since she spragged 'im last time that they met—

Jim ain't inlisted—but 'e's thinkin' 'ard.
Mick wus 'er 'ero long before the war,
An' now 'e's sort o' chalked a double score.

That's all Sir Garneo. But Mick, 'e's vowed
    This " 'Ail the 'Ero" stunt gits on 'is nerves,
An' makes 'im peevish; tho' 'e owns 'is crowd
    Can mop up all the praises they deserves.
"But don't yeh spread the 'ero on too thick
If it's exhaustin' yeh," sez Ginger Mick.

"We ain't got no objections to the cheers;
    We're good an' tough, an' we can stand the noise;
But three 'oorays and five or six long beers
    An' loud remarks about 'Our Gallant Boys'
Sounds kind o' weak—if you'll ixcuse the word—
Beside the fightin' sounds we've lately 'eard.

"If you'll fergive our blushes, we can stand
    The 'earty cheerin' an' the songs o' praise.
The loud 'Osannas uv our native land
    Makes us feel good an' glad in many ways.
An' later, when we land back in a mob,
Per'aps we might be arstin' fer a job.

"I'd 'ate," sez Mick, "to 'ave you think us rude,
    Or take these few remarks as reel bad taste;
'Twould 'urt to 'ave it seem ingratichude,
    Wiv all them 'earty praises gone to waste.
We'll take yer word fer it, an' jist remark
This 'ero racket is a reel good lark.

"Once, when they caught me toppin' off a John,
    The Bench wus stern, an' torked uv dirty work;

But, 'Struth! it's bonzer 'ow me fame's come on
    Since when I took to toppin' off the Turk.
So, if it pleases, shout yer loud 'Bravoes,'
An' later—don't fergit there's me, an' Rose."

So Ginger writes. I gives it word fer word;
    An' if it ain't the nice perlite reply
That nice, perlite old gents would liked to've 'eard
    'Oo've been 'ip-'ippin' 'im up to the sky—
Well, I dunno, I s'pose 'e's gotter learn
It's rude fer 'im to speak out uv 'is turn.

'Eroes. It sounds a bit of reel orl-right—
    "Our Gallant 'Eroes of Gallipoli."
But Ginger, when 'e's thinkin' there at night,
    Uv Rose, an' wot their luck is like to be
After the echo dies uv all this praise,
Well—'e ain't dazzled wiv three loud 'oorays.

A LETTER TO THE FRONT

I 'AVE written Mick a letter in reply to one uv 'is,
Where 'e arsts 'ow things is goin' where the gums an' wattles is.
So I tries to buck 'im up a bit; to go fer Abdul's fez;
An' I ain't no nob at litrachure; but this is wot I sez:

I suppose you fellers dream, Mick, in between the scraps out there,
Uv the land yeh left be'ind yeh when yeh sailed to do yer share:
Uv Collins Street, or Rundle Street, or Pitt, or George, or Hay,
Uv the land beyond the Murray or along the Castlereagh.
An' I guess yeh dream of old days an' the things yeh used to do,
An' yeh wonder 'ow 'twill strike yeh when yeh've seen this business
thro',
An' yeh try to count yer chances when yeh've finished wiv the Turk
An' swap the gaudy war game fer a spell o' plain, drab work.

Well, Mick, yeh know jist 'ow it is these early days o' Spring,
When the gildin' o' the wattle chucks a glow on ev'rything.
Them olden days, the golden days that you remember well,
In spite o' war an' worry, Mick, are wiv us fer a spell.
Fer the green is on the paddicks, an' the sap is in the trees,
An' the bush birds in the gullies sing the ole, sweet melerdies;
An' we're 'opin', as we 'ear 'em, that, when next the Springtime comes,
You'll be wiv us 'ere to listen to that bird tork in the gums.

It's much the same ole Springtime, Mick, yeh reckerlect uv yore;
Boronier an' dafferdils and wattle blooms once more

Sling sweetness over city streets, an' seem to put to shame
The rotten greed an' butchery that got you on this game—
The same ole sweet September days, an' much the same ole place;
Yet, there's a sort o' *somethin'*, Mick, upon each passin' face,
A sort o' look that's got me beat; a look that you put there,
The day yeh lobbed upon the beach an' charged at Sari Bair.

It isn't that we're boastin', lad; we've done wiv most o' that—
The froth, the cheers, the flappin' flags, the giddy wavin' 'at.
Sich things is childish memories; we blush to 'ave 'em told,
Fer we 'ave seen our wounded, Mick, an' it 'as made us old.
We ain't growed soggy wiv regret, we ain't swelled out wiv pride;
 But we 'ave seen it's up to us to lay our toys aside.
An' it wus you that taught us, Mick, we've growed too old fer play,
An' everlastin' picter shows, an' goin' down the Bay.

An', as a grown man dreams at times uv boy'ood days gone by,
So, when we're feelin' crook, I s'pose, we'll sometimes sit an' sigh.
But as a clean lad takes the ring wiv mind an' 'eart serene,
So I am 'opin' we will fight to make our man'ood clean.
When orl the stoushin's over, Mick, there's 'eaps o' work to do:
An' in the peaceful scraps to come we'll still be needin' you.
We will be needin' you the more fer wot yeh've seen an' done;
Fer you were born a Builder, lad, an' we 'ave jist begun.

There's bin a lot o' tork, ole mate, uv wot we owe to you,
An' wot yeh've braved an' done fer us, an' wot we mean to do.
We've 'ailed you boys as 'eroes, Mick, an' torked uv just reward
When you 'ave done the job yer at an' slung aside the sword.
I guess it makes yeh think a bit, an' weigh this gaudy praise;
Fer even 'eroes 'ave to eat, an'—there is other days:
The days to come when we don't need no bonzer boys to fight:
When the flamin's picnic's over an' the Leeuwin looms in sight.

Then there's another fight to fight, an' you will find it tough
To sling the Kharki clobber fer the plain civilian stuff.
When orl the cheerin' dies away, an' 'ero-worship flops,
Yeh'll 'ave to face the ole tame life—'ard yakker or 'ard cops,
But, lad, yer land is wantin' yeh, an' wantin' each strong son
To fight the fight that never knows the firin' uv a gun:
The steady fight, when orl you boys will show wot you are worth,
An' punch a cow on Yarra Flats or drive a quill in Perth.

The gilt is on the wattle, Mick, young leaves is on the trees,
An' the bush birds in the gullies swap the ole sweet melerdies,
There's a good, green land awaitin' you when you come 'ome again
To swing a pick at Ballarat or ride Yarrowie Plain.
The streets is gay wiv dafferdils—but—haggard in the sun,
A wounded soljer passes; an' we know ole days is done.
Fer somew'ere down inside us, lad, is somethin' you put there
The day yeh swung a dirty left, fer us, at Sari Bair.

RABBITS

"AR! Gimme fights wiv foemen I kin see,
    To upper-cut an' wallop on the jor.
Life in a burrer ain't no good to me.
        'Struth! This ain't war!
Gimme a ding-dong go fer 'arf a round,
An' you kin 'ave this crawlin' underground.

"Gimme a ragin', 'owlin', tearin' scrap,
    Wiv room to swing me left, an' feel it land.
This 'idin', sneakin' racket makes a chap
        Feel secon'-'and.
Stuck in me dug-out 'ere, down in a 'ole,
I'm feelin' like I've growed a rabbit's soul."

Ole Ginger's left the 'orspital, it seems;
    'E's back at Anzac, cursin' at the game;
Fer this 'ere ain't the fightin' uv 'is dreams;
        It's too dead tame.
'E's got the oopizootics reely bad,
An' 'idin' in a burrer makes 'im mad.

'E sort o' takes it personal, yeh see.
    'E used to 'awk 'em fer a crust, did Mick.
Now, makin' *im* play rabbits seems to be
        A narsty trick.

To shove 'im like a bunny down a 'ole
It looks like chuckin' orf, an' sours 'is soul.

"Fair doos," 'e sez. "I joined the bloomin' ranks
    To git away frum rabbits: thinks I'm done
Wiv them Australian pests, an' 'ere's their thanks:
        They makes me one!
An' 'ere I'm squattin', scared to shift about;
Jist waitin' fer me little tail to sprout.

"Ar, strike me up a wattle! but it's tough!
    But 'ere's the dizzy limit, fer a cert—
To live this bunny's life is bad enough,
        But 'ere's reel dirt:
Some tart at 'ome 'as sent, wiv lovin' care,
A coat uv rabbit-skins fer me to wear!

"That's done it! Now I'm nibblin' at me food,
    An' if a dawg shows up I'll start to squeal.
I s'pose I orter melt wiv gratichude:
        'Tain't 'ow I feel.
She might 'a' fixed a note on wiv a pin:
'Please, Mister Rabbit, yeh fergot yer skin!'

"I sees me finish! ... War? Why, this ain't war!
    It's ferritin'! An' I'm the bloomin' game.
Me skin alone is worth the 'untin' for—
        That tart's to blame!
Before we're done, I've got a silly scare,
Some trappin' Turk will catch me in a snare.

" 'E'll skin me, wiv the others 'e 'as there,
    An' shove us on a truck, an' bung us 'round
Constantinople at a bob a pair—

'Orl fresh an' sound!
'Eads down, 'eels up, 'e'll 'awk us in a row
Around the 'arems, 'owlin' 'Rabbee-oh!'

"But, dead in earnest, it's a job I 'ate.
     We've got to do it, an' it's gittin' done;
But this soul-dopin' game uv sit-an'-wait
          It ain't no fun.
There's times I wish, if we weren't short uv men,
That I wus back in 'orspital again.

"Ar, 'orspital! There is the place to git.
     If I thort Paradise wus 'arf so snug
I'd shove me 'ead above the parapit
          An' stop a slug.
But one thing blocks me playin' sich a joke:
I want another scrap before I croak.

"I want it bad. I want to git right out
     An' plug some josser in the briskit—'ard.
I want to 'owl an' chuck me arms about,
          An' jab, an' guard,
An' swing, an' upper-cut, an' crool some pitch,
Or git passed out meself—I don't care w'ich.

"There's some blokes 'ere they've tumbled to a stunt
     Fer gittin' 'em the spell that they deserves.
They chews some cordite when life at the front
          Gits on their nerves.
It sends yer tempracher clean out uv sight,
An', if yeh strike a simple doc, yer right.

"I tries it once. Me soul 'ad got the sinks,
     Me thorts annoyed me, an' I 'ad the joes,

I feels like no one loves me, so I thinks,
  Well, Mick, 'ere goes!
I breaks a cartridge open, chews a bit,
Reports I'm sick, an' throws a fancy fit.

"Me lovin' sargint spreads the gloomy noos,
  I gits paraded; but, aw, 'Struth! me luck!
It weren't no baby doc I interviews,
   But some ole buck
Wiv gimblet eyes. 'Put out yer tongue!' 'e 'owls.
Then takes me temp, an' stares at me, an' growls.

" 'Well, well,' 'e sez. 'Wot is yer trouble, lad?'
  I grabs me tummy 'ard, an' sez I'm ill.
'You are,' sez 'e. 'Yeh got corditis, bad.
   Yeh need a pill.
Before yeh go to sleep,' 'e sez, 'to-night,
Swaller the bullet, son, an' you'll be right.'

" 'Ow's that fer rotten luck? But orl the same,
  I ain't complainin' when I thinks it out.
I seen it weren't no way to play the game,
   This pullin' out.
We're orl uv us in this to see it thro',
An' bli'me, wot we've got to do, we'll do.

"But 'oles an' burrers! Strike! An' this is war!
  This is the bonzer scrappin' uv me dreams!
A willin' go is wot I bargained for,
   But 'ere it seems
I've died, someway, an' bin condemned to be
Me own Wile Rabbee fer eternity.

"But 'orspital! I tell yeh, square an' all,
    If I could meet the murderin' ole Turk
'Oo's bullet sent me there to loaf an' sprawl,
      An' dodge me work,
Lord! I'd shake 'an's wiv 'im, an' thank 'im well
Fer givin' me a reel ole bonzer spell.

" 'E might 'a' made it jist a wee bit worse.
    I'd stand a lot uv that before I'd scream.
The grub wus jist the thing; an', say, me nurse!
    She wus a dream!
I used to treat them tony tarts wiv mirth;
But now I know why they wus put on earth.

"It treated me reel mean, that wound uv mine;
    It 'ealed too quick, considerin' me state.
An' 'ere I am, back in the firin' line
      Gamblin' wiv Fate.
It's like two-up: I'm 'eadin' 'em this trip;
But lookin', day be day, to pass the kip.

"You tell Doreen, yer wife, 'ow I am chock
    Full to the neck wiv thanks fer things she sends.
Each time I shoves me foot inside a sock
    I bless sich friends.
I'm bustin' wiv glad thorts fer things she did;
So tell 'er I serloots 'er, an' the kid.

"Make 'im a soljer, chum, when 'e gits old.
    Teach 'im the tale uv wot the Anzacs did.
Teach 'im 'e's got a land to love an' hold.
    Gawd bless the kid!
But I'm in 'opes when 'is turn comes around
They'll chuck this style uv rootin' underground.

"We're up agin it, mate; we know that well.
    There ain't a man among us wouldn't lob
Over the parapit an' charge like 'ell
        To end the job.
But this is war; an' discipline—well, lad,
We sez we 'ates it; but we ain't too bad.

"Glory an' gallant scraps is wot I dreamed,
    Ragin' around an' smashin' foemen flat;
But war, like other things, ain't wot it seems.
        So 'stid uv that,
I'm sittin' in me dug-out scrawlin' this,
An' thankin' Gawd when shells go by—an' miss.

"I'm sittin' in me dug-out day be day—
    It narks us; but Australia's got a name
Fer doin' little jobs like blokes 'oo play
        A clean, straight game.
Wiv luck I might see scrappin' 'fore I'm done,
Or go where Craig 'as gone, an' miss the fun.

"But if I dodge, an' keep out uv the rain,
    An' don't toss in me alley 'fore we wins;
An' if I lobs back 'ome an' meets the Jane
        'Oo sent the skins—
These bunnies' overcoats I lives inside—
I'll squeal at 'er, an' run away an' 'ide.

"But, torkin' straight, the Janes 'as done their bit.
    I'd like to 'ug the lot, orl on me pat!
They warms us well, the things they've sewed an' knit:
        An' more than that—
I'd like to tell them dear Australian tarts
The spirit uv it warms Australian 'earts."

TO THE BOYS WHO TOOK THE COUNT

SEE, I'm writin' to Mick as a bloke to a bloke—
    To a cobber o' mine at the front—
An' I'm gittin' full up uv the mullock they poke
    At the cove that is bearin' the brunt.
Fer 'e mus'n't do this an' 'e shouldn't do that,
    An' 'e's crook if 'e looks a bit shick,
An' 'e's gittin' too uppish, an' don't touch 'is 'at—
    But 'ere's 'ow I puts it to Mick.

Now, it's dickin to style if yer playin' the game,
    If it's marbles, or shinty, or war;
I've seen 'em lob 'ome 'ere, the 'alt an' the lame,
    That wus fine 'efty fellers before.
They wus toughs, they wus crooks, they wus ev'ry bad thing,
    But they mixed it as gentlemen should.
So 'ere's to the coot wiv 'is eye in a sling,
    An' a smile in the one that is good.

It wus playin' the game in the oval an' ring —
    An' playin' fer orl it wus worth—
That give 'em the knack uv a punch wiv a sting
    When they fought fer the land uv their birth.
They wus pebs, they wus narks, they wus reel naughty boys,
    But they didn't need no second 'int,
So ere's to the bloke wiv 'is swearin' an' noise,
    An' 'is foot in a fathom uv lint.

There wus fellers I knoo in the soft days uv peace;
    An' I didn't know much to their good;
An' they give more 'ard graft to the overworked p'leece
    Than a reel puffick gentleman should.
They wus lookin' fer lash long before it wus doo;
    When it come, they wus into it, straight.
So 'ere's to the bloke wiv 'is shoulder shot thro'
    'Oo is cursin' the days 'e's to wait.

Ar, dickin to swank! when it comes to a mill,
    It's the bloke wiv a punch 'oo's yer friend.
An' a coarse, narsty man wiv the moniker Bill
    Earns the thanks uv the crowd in the end.
(An' when I sez "earns" I am 'opin' no stint
    Will be charged agin us by-an'-bye.)
So, 'ere's to the boy wiv 'is arm in a splint
    An' a "don't-care-a-dam" in 'is eye.

'Cos the fightin's too far fer to give us a grip
    Of the 'ell full uv slaughter an' noise,
There's a breed that gives me the pertickler pip
    Be the way that they torks uv the boys.
O, they're coarse, an' they're rude, an' it's awful to live
    Wiv their cursin' an' shoutin' an' fuss.
Dam it! 'Ere's to the bloke wiv the bad-lookin' chiv
    That 'e poked inter trouble fer us!

O, it's dead agin etikit, dead agin style
    Fer to swear an' to swagger an' skite;
But a battle ain't won wiv a drorin'-room smile,
    An' yeh 'ave to be rude in a fight.
An' it's bein' reel rude to enemy blokes
    That'll earn yeh that 'ero-like touch,

So 'ere's to the boy wiv 'is curses an' jokes
    'Oo is 'oppin' about on a crutch.

Now, the Turk is a gent, an' they greets 'im as such,
    An' they gives doo respect to 'is Nibs;
But 'e never 'eld orf to apolergise much
    When 'e slid 'is cold steel in their ribs.
An' our boys won the name that they give 'em of late
    'Cos they fought like a jugful uv crooks,
So 'ere's to the bloke wiv the swaggerin' gait
    An' a bullet mark spoilin' 'is looks.

So, the bloke wiv the scoff, an' the bloke wiv the sneer,
    An' the coot wiv the sensitive soul,
'E 'as got to sit back, an' jist change 'is idear
    Uv the stuffin' that makes a man whole.
Fer the polish an' gilt that's a win wiv the skirts
    It wears thin wiv the friction uv war.
So, 'ere's to the cove 'oo is nursin' 'is 'urts
    Wiv an oath in the set uv 'is jor.

When yeh've stripped a cove clean an' got down to the buff
    Yeh come to the meat that's the man.
If yeh want to find grit an' sich similar stuff,
    Yeh've to strip on a similar plan.
Fer there's nothin' like scrappin' to bare a man's soul,
    If it's Billo, or Percy, or Gus.
So 'ere's to the bloke 'oo 'ops round on a pole
    An' 'owls songs goin' 'ome on the bus.

Spare me days! When a bloke takes the count in a scrap
    That 'e's fightin' fer you an' fer me,
Is it fair that a snob 'as the nerve fer to snout
    Any swad 'cos 'is manners is free?

They're deservin' our thanks, frum the best to the worst—
    An' there's some is reel rorty, I own—
But 'ere's to the coot wiv the 'ang-over thirst
    'Oo sprags a stray toff fer a loan.

So I'm writin' to Mick; an' I'm feelin' reel wet
    Wiv the sort o' superior nark,
'Oo tilts up 'is conk an' gits orl the boys set,
    'Oo are out fer a bit uv a lark.
So I puts it to Mick, as I sez when I starts,
    An' I ends wiv the solemest toast:
'Ere's to 'im—(raise yer glass)—'oo left pride in our 'earts
    An' 'is bones on Gallipoli coast.

THE GAME

"HO! the sky's as blue as blazes an' the sun is shinin' bright,
    An' the dicky birds is singin' over 'ead,
An' I'm 'ummin', softly 'ummin', w'ile I'm achin' fer a fight,
    An' the chance to fill some blighter full o' lead.
An' the big guns they are boomin', an' the shells is screamin' past,
But I'm corperil—lance-corperil, an' found me game at last!"

I ixpects a note frum Ginger, fer the time wus gettin' ripe,
An' I gits one thick wiv merry 'owls uv glee,
Fer they've gone an' made 'im corperil—they've given 'im a stripe,
    An' yeh'd think, to see 'is note, it wus V.C.
Fer 'e chortles like a nipper wiv a bran' noo Noer's Ark
Since Forchin she 'as smiled on 'im, an' life's no more a nark.

"Ho! the sky along the 'ill-tops, it is smudged wiv cannon smoke,
    An' the shells along the front is comin' fast,
But the 'eads 'ave 'ad the savvy fer to reckernise a bloke,
    An' permotion's gettin' common-sense at last.
An' they picked me fer me manners, w'ich wus snouted over 'ome,
But I've learned to be a soljer since I crossed the ragin' foam.

"They 'ave picked me 'cos they trust me; an' it's got me where I live,
    An' it's put me on me metal, square an' all.
I wusn't in the runnin' once when blokes 'ad trust to give,
    But over 'ere I answers to the call.

So some shrewd 'ead 'e marked me well, an' when the time wus ripe,
'E took a chance on Ginger Mick, an' I 'ave snared me stripe.

"I know wot I wus born fer now, an' soljerin's me game,
    That's no furphy; but I never guessed it once;
Fer when I 'it things up at 'ome they said I wus to blame,
    An' foolish beaks they sent me up fer munce.
But 'ere—well, things is different to wot sich things wus then,
Fer me game is playin' soljers, an' me lurk is 'andlin' men.

"Me game is 'andlin' men, orl right, I seen it in the parst
    When I used to 'ead the pushes in the Lane.
An' ev'ry bloke among 'em then done everythin' I arst,
    Fer I never failed to make me meanin' plain.
Disturbers uv the peace we wus them days, but now I know
We wus aimin' to be soljers, but we never 'ad a show.

"We never 'ad no discipline, that's wot we wanted bad,
    It's discipline that gives the push its might.
But wot a time we could 'ave give the coppers if we 'ad,
    Lord! We'd 'ave capchered Melbourne in a night.
When I think uv things that might 'ave been I sometimes sit an' grin,
Fer I might be King uv Footscray if we'd 'ad more discipline.

"I've got a push to 'andle now wot makes a soljer proud.
    Yeh ort to see the boys uv my ole squad.
The willin'est, the cheeriest, don'-care-a-damest crowd
    An' the toughest ever seen outside o' quod.
I reckon that they gimme 'em becos they wus so meek,
But they know me, an' they understan' the lingo that I speak.

"So I'm a little corperil, wiv pretties on me arm,
    But yeh'd never guess it fer to see me now,
Fer me valet 'e's been careless an' me trooso's come to 'arm,

An' me pants want creasin' badly I'll allow.
But to see me squad in action is a cure fer sandy blight,
They are shy on table manners, but they've notions 'ow ter fight.

"There's a little picnic promised that 'as long been overdoo,
    An' we're waitin' fer the order to advance;
An' me bones is fairly achin' fer to see my boys bung thro',
    Fer I know they're dancin' mad to git the chance.
An' there's some'll sure be missin' when we git into the game;
But if they lorst their corperil 'twould be a cryin' shame.

"We can't afford no corperils. But, some'ow, I dunno,
    I got a nervis feelin' in me chest,
That this 'ere bit uv fancy work might be me final go
    An' I won't be 'ome to dinner wiv the rest.
It's rot; but it keeps comin' back, that lonely kind o' mood
That fills me up wiv mushy thorts that don't do any good.

"When it's gettin' near to evenin' an' the guns is slowin' down
    I fergits the playful 'abits uv our foes,
An' finds meself a-thinkin' thorts uv good ole Melbourne town,
    An' dreamin' dilly dreams about ole Rose.
O' course I'll see me girl again, an' give a clean, square deal,
When I come smilin' 'ome again ... But that ain't 'ow I feel.

"I feel ... I dunno 'ow I feel. I feel that things is done.
    I seem t've 'it the limit in some way.
Per'aps I'm orf me pannikin wiv sittin' in the sun,
    But I jist wrote to Rose the other day.
An' I wrote 'er sort o' mournful 'cos—I dunno 'ow it seems ...
Ar, I'm a gay galoot to go an' 'ave these dilly dreams!

"Wot price the bran' noo corperil, wiv sof'nin' uv the 'eart!
    If my pet lambs thort me a turtle dove

I'd 'ave to be reel stern wiv 'em, an' make another start
      To git 'em where I got 'em jist wiv love …
But don't fergit, if you or your Doreen sees Rose about,
Jist tell 'er that I'm well an' strong, an' sure uv winnin' out.

"Ho! the sky's as blue as blazes, an' the sun is shinin' still,
      An' the dicky bird is perchin' on the twig,
An' the guns is pop, pop, poppin' frum the trenches on the 'ill,
      An' I'm lookin' bonny in me non-com's rig.
An' when yer writin' me again—don't think I want ter skite—
But don't fergit the 'Corperil'; an' mind yeh spells it right."

'A GALLANT GENTLEMAN'

A MONTH ago the world grew grey fer me;
    A month ago the light went out fer Rose.
To 'er they broke it gentle as might be;
    But fer 'is pal 'twus one uv them swift blows
That stops the 'eart-beat; fer to me it came
Jist, "Killed in Action," an', beneath, 'is name.

'Ow many times 'ave I sat dreamin' 'ere
    An' seen the boys returning', gay an' proud.
I've seen the greetin's, 'eard 'is rousin' cheer,
    An' watched ole Mick come stridin' thro' the crowd.
'Ow many times 'ave I sat in this chair
An' seen 'is 'ard chiv grinnin' over there.

'E's laughed, an' told me stories uv the war.
    Changed some 'e looked, but still the same ole Mick,
Keener an' cleaner than 'e wus before.
    'E's took me 'and, an' said 'e's in great nick.
Sich wus the dreamin's uv a fool 'oo tried
To jist crack 'ardy, an' 'old gloom aside.

An' now—well, wot's the odds? I'm only one:
    One out uv many 'oo 'as lost a friend.
Manlike, I'll bounce again, an' find me fun;
    But fer poor Rose it seems the bitter end.

Fer Rose, an' sich as Rose, when one man dies
It seems the world goes black before their eyes.

Fer Rose, an' sich as Rose, thro' orl the world,
    War piles the burdens wiv a 'eavy 'and.
Since bugles called an' banners were unfurled,
    A sister'ood 'as growed thro' orl the land—
A 'oly sister'ood that puts aside
Sham things, an' 'and takes 'and in grief—an' pride.

Ar, well; if Mick could 'ear me blither now,
    I know jist wot 'e'd say an' 'ow 'e'd look:
"Aw, cut it out, mate; chuck that silly row!
    There ain't no sense in takin' sich things crook.
I've took me gamble; an' there's none to blame
Becos I drew a blank; it's in the game."

A parson cove he broke the noos to Rose—
    A friend uv mine, a bloke wiv snowy 'air,
An' gentle, soothin' sort o' ways, 'oo goes
    Thro' life jist 'umpin' others' loads uv care.
Instid uv Mick—jist one rough soljer lad—
Yeh'd think 'e'd lost the dearest friend 'e 'ad.

But 'ow kin blows be sof'n'd sich as that?
    Rose took it as 'er sort must take sich things.
An' if the jolt uv it 'as knocked me flat,
    Well, 'oo is there to blame 'er if it brings
Black thorts that comes to women when they frets,
An' makes 'er tork wild tork an' foolish threats.

An' then there come the letter that wus sent
    To give the strength uv Ginger's passin' out—
A long, straight letter frum a bloke called Trent.

'Tain't no use tellin' wot it's orl about.
There's things that's in it I kin see quite clear
Ole Ginger Mick ud be ashamed to 'ear.

Things praisin' 'im, that pore ole Mick ud say
    Wus comin' it too 'ot; fer, spare me days!
I well remember that 'e 'ad a way
    Uv curlin' up when 'e wus slung bokays.
An' Trent 'e seems to think that in some way
'E owes Mick somethin' that 'e can't repay.

Well, p'raps 'e does; an' in the note 'e sends
    'E arsts if Mick 'as people 'e kin find.
Fer Trent's an English toff wiv swanky friends,
    An' wants to 'elp wot Ginger's left be'ind.
'E sez strange things in this 'ere note 'e sends:
"He was a gallant gentleman," it ends.

A gallant gentleman! Well, I dunno.
    I 'ardly think that Mick ud like that name.
But this 'ere Trent's a toff, an' ort to know
    The breedin' uv the stock frum which 'e came.
Gallant an' game Mick might 'a' bin; but then—
Lord! Fancy 'im among the gentlemen!

'E wus a man; that's good enough fer me,
    'Oo wus 'is cobber many years before
'E writ it plain fer other blokes to see,
    An' proved it good an' plenty at the war.
'E wus a man; an', by the way 'e died,
'E wus a man 'is friend kin claim wiv pride.

The way 'e died … Gawd! but it makes me proud
    I ever 'eld 'is 'and, to read that tale.

An' Trent is one uv that 'igh-steppin' crowd
    That don't sling praise around be ev'ry mail.
To 'im it seemed some great 'eroic lurk;
But Mick, I know, jist took it wiv 'is work.

No matter wot 'e done. It's jist a thing
    I knoo 'e'd do if once 'e got the show.
An' it would never please 'im fer to sling
    Tall tork at 'im jist 'cos 'e acted so.
"Don't make a song uv it!" I 'ear 'im growl,
"I've done me limit, an' tossed in the tow'l."

This little job, 'e knoo—an' I know well—
    A thousand uv 'is cobbers would 'ave done.
Fer they are soljers; an' it's crook to tell
    A tale that marks fer praise a single one.
An' that's 'ow Mick would 'ave it, as I know;
An', as 'e'd 'ave it, so we'll let it go.

Trent tells 'ow, when they found 'im, near the end,
    'E starts a fag an' grins orl bright an' gay.
An' when they arsts fer messages to send
    To friends, 'is look goes dreamin' far away.
"Look after Rose," 'e sez, "when I move on.
Look after … Rose … Mafeesh!" An' e' wus gone.

"We buried 'im," sez Trent, "down by the beach.
    We put mimosa on the mound uv sand
Above 'im. 'Twus the nearest thing in reach
    To golden wattle uv 'is native land.
But never wus the fairest wattle wreath
More golden than the 'eart uv 'im beneath."

An' so—Mafeesh! as Mick 'ad learned to say.
　　'E's finished; an' there's few 'as marked 'im go.
Only one soljer, outed in the fray,
　　'Oo took 'is gamble, an' 'oo 'ad 'is show.
There's few to mourn 'im: an' the less they leave,
The less uv sorrer; fewer 'earts to grieve.

An' when I'm feelin' blue, an' mopin' 'ere
　　About the pal I've lorst; Doreen, my wife,
She come an' takes my 'and, an' tells me, "Dear,
　　There'd be more cause to mourn a wasted life.
'E proved 'imself a man; an' 'e's at rest."
An' so, I tries to think sich things is best.

A gallant gentleman … Well, let it go.
　　They sez they've put them words above is 'ead,
Out there where lonely graves stretch in a row;
　　But Mick 'e'll never mind it now 'e's dead.
An' where 'e's gone, when they weigh praise an' blame,
P'raps gentlemen an' men is much the same.

They fights; an' orl the land is filled wiv cheers.
　　They dies; an' 'ere an' there a 'eart is broke.
An' when I weighs it orl—the shouts, the tears—
　　I sees it's well Mick wus a lonely bloke.
'E found a game 'e knoo, an' played it well;
An' now 'e's gone. Wot more is there to tell?

A month ago, fer me the world grew grey;
　　A month ago the light went out fer Rose;
Becos one common soljer crossed the way,
　　Leavin' a common message as 'e goes.
But ev'ry dyin' soljer's 'ope lies there:
"Look after Rose. Mafeesh!" Gawd! It's a pray'r!

That's wot it is; an' when yeh sort it out,
  Shuttin' yer ears to orl the sounds o' strife—
The shouts, the cheers, the curses—'oo kin doubt
  The claims uv women: mother, sweet'eart, wife?
An' 'oo's to 'ear our soljers' dyin' wish?
An' 'oo's to 'eed? … "Look after Rose … Mafeesh!"

Glossary

For use with *The Sentimental Bloke* and *Ginger Mick*.

A.I.F.—Australian Imperial Forces.

Alley, to toss in the.—To give up the ghost.

Also ran, The.—On the turf, horses that fail to secure a leading place; hence, obscure persons, nonentities.

'Ammer-lock (Hammer-lock).—A favourite and effective hold in wrestling.

Ar.—An exclamation expressing joy, sorrow, surprise, etc., according to the manner of utterance.

'Ard Case (Hard Case).—A shrewd or humorous person.

'Ayseed (Hayseed).—A rustic.

Back Chat.—Impudent repartee.

Back and Fill.—To vacillate; to shuffle.

Back the Barrer.—To intervene without invitation.

Barmy (Balmy).—Foolish; silly.

Beak.—A magistrate. (Possibly from Anglo-Saxon, Beag—a magistrate).

Beano.—A feast.

Beans.—Coins; money.

Beat.—Puzzled; defeated.

Beat, off the.—Out of the usual routine.

Beef (to beef it out).—To declaim vociferously.

Bellers (Bellows).—The lungs.

Biff.—To smite.

Bird, to give the.—To treat with derision.

Blighter.—A worthless fellow.

Bli' me.—An oath with the fangs drawn.

Blither.—To talk at random, foolishly.

Blob.—A shapeless mass.

Block.—The head. To lose or do in the block.—To become flustered; excited; angry; to lose confidence. To keep the block.—To remain calm; dispassionate.

Block, the.—A fashionable city walk.

Bloke.—A male adult of the genus homo.

Blubber, blub.—To weep.

Bluff.—Cunning practice; make believe. v. To deceive; to mislead.

Bob.—A shilling.

Bokays.—Compliments, flattery.

Boko.—The nose.

Bonzer, boshter, bosker.—Adjectives expressing the superlative of excellence.

Bong-tong.—Patrician (Fr. bon ton).

Boodle.—Money; wealth.

Book.—A bookie, q.v.

Bookie.—A book-maker (turf); one who makes a betting book on sporting events.

Boot, to put in the.—To kick a prostrate foe.

Boss.—Master; employer.

Break (to break away, to do a break).—To depart in haste.

Breast up to.—To accost.

Brisket.—The chest.

Brown.—A copper coin.

Brums.—Tawdry finery (from Brummagem—Birmingham).

Buckley's (Chance).—A forlorn hope.

Buck up.—Cheer up.

Bump.—To meet; to accost aggressively.

Bun, to take the.—To take the prize (used ironically).

Bundle, to drop the.—To surrender; to give up hope.

Bunk.—To sleep in a "bunk" or rough bed. To do a bunk.—To depart.

Bunnies, to hawk the.—To peddle rabbits.

Bus, to miss the.—To neglect opportunities.

Caboose.—A small dwelling.

Carlton.—A Melbourne Football Team.

Cat, to whip the.—To cry over spilt milk; i.e., to whip the cat that has spilt the milk.

C.B.—Confined to barracks.

Cert.—A certainty; a foregone conclusion.

Champeen.—Champion.

Chase yourself.—Depart; avaunt; "fade away." q.v.

Chat.—To address tentatively; to "word," q.v.

Cheque, to pass in one's.—To depart this life.

Chest, to get it off one's.—To deliver aspeech; express one's feelings.

Chew, to chew it over; to chew the rag.—To sulk; to nurse a grievance.

Chiack.—Vulgar banter; coarse invective.

Chin.—To talk; to wag the chin.

Chip.—To "chat," q.v. Chip in.—To intervene.

Chiv.—The face.

Chow.—A native of far Cathay.

Chuck up.—To relinquish. Chuck off.—To chaff; to employ sarcasm.

Chump.—A foolish fellow.

Chunk.—A lump; a mass.

Clean.—Completely; utterly.

Click.—A clique; a "push."

Cliner.—A young unmarried female.

Clobber.—Raiment; vesture.

Cobber.—A boon companion.

Collect.—To receive one's deserts.

Colour-line.—In pugilism, the line drawn by white boxers excluding coloured fighters—for divers reasons.

Conk.—The nose.

Coot.—A person of no account (used contemptuously).

Cop.—To seize; to secure; also s., an avocation, a "job."

Cop (or Copper).—A police constable.

Copper-top.—Red head.

Copper show.—A copper mine.

Count, to take the.—In pugilism, to remain prostrate for ten counted seconds, and thus lose the fight.

Cove.—A "chap" or "bloke." q.v. (Gipsy).

Cow.—A thoroughly unworthy, not to say despicable person, place, thing or circumstance.

Crack.—To smite. s. A blow.

Crack a boo.—To divulge a secret; to betray emotion.

Crack hardy.—To suppress emotion; to endure patiently; to keep a secret.

Cray.—A crayfish.

Crib.—A dwelling.

Croak.—To die.

Crook.—A dishonest or evil person.

Crook.—Unwell; dishonest; spurious; fraudulent. Superlative, Dead Crook.

Crool (cruel) the pitch.—To frustrate; to interfere with one's schemes or welfare.

Crust.—Sustenance; a livelihood.

Cut it out.—Omit it; discontinue it.

Dago.—A native of Southern Europe.

Dash, to do one's.—To reach one's Waterloo.

Date.—An appointment.

Dawg (dog).—A contemptible person; ostentation. To put on dawg.—To behave in an arrogant manner.

Dead.—In a superlative degree; very.

Deal.—To deal it out; to administer punishment; abuse, etc.

Deener.—A shilling (Fr. Denier. Denarius, a Roman silver coin).

Derry.—An aversion; a feud; a dislike.

Dickin.—A term signifying disgust or disbelief.

Dile (dial).—The face.

Dilly.—Foolish; half-witted.

Ding Dong.—Strenuous.

Dinkum.—Honest; true. "The Dinkum Oil."—The truth.

Dirt.—Opprobrium, a mean speech or action.

Dirty left.—A formidable left fist.

Divvies.—Dividends; profits.

Dizzy limit.—The utmost; the superlative degree.

Do in.—To defeat; to kill; to spend.

Done me luck.—Lost my good fortune.

Dope.—A drug; adulterated liquor. v. To administer drugs.

Dot in the eye, to.—To strike in the eye.

Douse.—To extinguish (Anglo-Saxon).

Drive a quill.—To write with a pen; to work in an office.

Duck, to do a.—(See "break.")

Duds.—Personal apparel (Scotch).

Dunno.—Do not know.

Dutch.—German; any native of Central Europe.

'Eads (Heads).—The authorities; inner council.

'Eadin'.—"Heading browns;" tossing pennies.

'Ead over Turkey.—Heels over head.

'Ead Serang.—The chief; the leader.

'Eavyweight.—A boxer of the heaviest class.

'Ell fer leather.—In extreme haste.

End up, to get.—To raise to one's feet.

Fade away, to.—To retire; to withdraw.

Fag.—A cigarette.

Fair.—Extreme; positive.

Fair thing.—A wise proceeding; an obvious duty.

Fake.—A swindle; a hoax.

Finger.—An eccentric or amusing person.

Flam.—Nonsense, makebelieve.

Flash.—Ostentatious; showy but counterfeit.

Float, to.—To give up the ghost.

Fluff, a bit of.—A young female person.

Foot (me foot).—A term expressing ridicule.

Footer.—Football.

Frame.—The body.

Frill.—Affectation.

Funk, to.—To fear; to lose courage.

Furphy.—An idle rumour; a canard.

Galoot.—A simpleton.

Game.—Occupation; scheme; design.

Gawsave.—The National Anthem.

Gazob.—A fool; a blunderer.

Geewhizz.—Exclamation expressing surprise,

Get, to do a.—To retreat hastily.

Gilt.—Money; wealth.

Give, to.—In one sense, to care.

Gizzard.—The heart.

Glarssy.—The glassy eye; a glance of cold disdain. The Glassey Alley.—The favourite; the most admired.

Glim.—A light.

Going (while the going is good).—While the path is clear.

Gone (fair gone).—Overcome, as with emotion.

Goo-goo eyes.—Loving glances.

Gorspil-cove.—A minister of the Gospel.

Graft.—Work.

Grafter.—One who toils hard or willingly.

Griffin, the straight.—The truth; secret information.

Grip.—Occupation; employment.

Groggy.—Unsteady; dazed.

Grouch.—To mope; to grumble.

Grub.—Food.

Guff.—Nonsense.

Guy.—A foolish fellow.

Guy, to do a.—To retire.

Guyver.—Make-believe.

Handies.—A fondling of hands between lovers.

Hang out.—To reside; to last.

Hang-over.—The aftermath of the night before.

Hankies.—Handkerchiefs.

High-falutin'.—High sounding; boastful.

Hitch, to.—To wed.

Hitched.—Entangled in the bonds of holy matrimony.

Hit things up.—To behave strenuously; riotously.

Hot.—Excessive; extreme.

Hump, the.—A fit of depression.

Hump, to.—To carry as a swag or other burden.

Imshee.—Begone; retreat; to take yourself off.

Intro.—Introduction; knock-down. q.v.

It (to be It).—To assume a position of supreme importance.

Jab.—To strike smartly.

Jane.—A woman.

Jiff.—A very brief period.

Job, to.—To smite.

Joes.—Melancholy thoughts.

John.—A policeman.

Joint, to jump the.—To assume command; to occupy the "joint," i.e., establishment, situation, place of business.

Jolt, to pass a.—To deliver a short, sharp blow.

Jor.—The jaw.

Jorb (job).—Avocation; employment.

Josser.—A simple fellow.

Jug.—A prison.

Keekin'.—Peeping.

Keeps, for.—For ever; permanently.

Kersplosh.—Splash.

Kid.—A child.

Kid, to.—To deceive; to persuade by flattery.

Kiddies.—Children.

Kid Stakes.—Pretence.

King Pin.—The leader; the person of chief importance.

Kip.—A small chip used for tossing pennies in the occult game of two-up.

Kipsie.—A house; the home.

Knob.—The head; one in authority.

Knock-down.—A ceremony insisted upon by ladies who decline to be "picked up"; a formal introduction.

Knock-out drops.—Drugged or impure liquor.

Knock-out punch.—A knock-down blow.

Knut.—A fop; a well-dressed idler.

Lark.—A practical joke; a sportive jest.

Lash.—Violence.

Ledding.—Leaden.

Leery.—Vulgar; low.

Leeuwin.—Cape Leeuwin on the South-West coast of Australia.

Lid.—The hat. To dip the lid.—To raise the hat.

Limit.—The end; the full length.

Line up.—To approach; to accost.

Lingo.—Language.

Lip.—Impertinence. To give it lip.—To talk vociferously.

Little Bourke.—Little Bourke Street, Melbourne, Australia.

Little Lons.—Little Lonsdale Street, Melbourne, Australia.

Lob, to.—To arrive.

'Loo.—Woolloomooloo, a part of Sydney.

Lumme.—Love me.

Lurk.—A plan of action; a regular occupation.

Mafeesh.—Finish; I am finished.

Mag.—To scold or talk noisily.

Mallee.—A species of Eucalypt; the country where the Mallee grows.

Mash.—To woo; to pay court. s. A lover.

Maul.—To lays hands upon, either violently or with affection.

Meet, a.—An assignation.

Mill.—A bout of fisticuffs.

Mix.—To mix it; to fight strenuously.

Mizzle.—To disappear; to depart suddenly.

Mo.—Abbreviation of "moment."

Moll.—A woman of loose character.

Moniker.—A name; a title; a signature.

Mooch.—To saunter about aimlessly.

Moon.—To loiter.

Mud, my name is.—i.e., I am utterly discredited.

Mug, to.—To kiss.

Mullock, to poke.—To deride; to tease.

Mushy.—Sentimental.

Nark.—s., a spoil-sport; a churlish fellow.

Nark, to.—To annoy; to foil.

Narked.—Angered; foiled.

Natchril.—Natural.

Neck, to get in the.—To receive severe punishment, i.e., "Where the chicken got the axe."

Nerve.—Confidence; impudence.

Nick.—Physical condition; good health.

Nipper.—A small boy.

Nose around, to.—To seek out inquisitively.

Nothing (ironically).—Literally "something considerable."

Odds, above the.—Beyond the average; outside the pale.

Oopizootics.—An undiagnosed complaint.

Orfis (office).—A warning; a word of advice; a hint.

Oricle (oracle), to work the.—To secure desired results.

Orl (all in).—Without limit or restriction.

'To Socks.—Gaily coloured hose.

Out, to.—To render unconscious with a blow.

Out, all.—Quite exhausted; fully extended.

Pack, to send to the.—To relegate to obscurity.

Pal.—A friend; a mate (Gipsy).

Pard.—A partner; a mate.

Pass (pass 'im one).—To deliver a blow.

Pat, on one's.—Alone; single-handed.

Peach.—A desirable young woman; "fresh as a peach."

Peb (pebble).—A flash fellow; a "larrikin."

Phiz.—The face.

Pick at.—To chaff; to annoy.

Pick up, to.—To dispense with the ceremony of a "knock-down" or introduction.

Pilot cove.—A clergyman.

Pile it on.—To rant; to exaggerate.

Pinch.—To steal; to place under arrest.

Pip.—A fit of depression.

Pitch a tale.—To trump up an excuse; to weave a romance.

Plant.—To bury.

Plug.—To smite with the fist.

Plug along, to.—To proceed doggedly.

Plunk.—An exclamation expressing the impact of a blow.

Podgy.—Fat; plump.

Point.—The region of the jaw; much sought after by pugilists.

Point, to.—To seize unfair advantage; to scheme.

Pole, up the.—Distraught through anger, fear, etc.; also, disappeared, vanished.

Pot, a.—A considerable amount; as a "pot of money."

Pot, the old.—The male parent (from "Rhyming Slang," the "old pot and pan"—the "old man.")

Prad.—A horse.

Pug.—A pugilist.

Pull, to take a.—To desist; to discontinue.

Punch a cow.—To conduct a team of oxen.

Punter.—The natural prey of a "bookie." q.v.

Push.—A company of rowdy fellows gathered together for ungentle purposes.

Queer the pitch.—To frustrate; to fool.

Quid.—A sovereign, or pound sterling.

Quod.—Prison.

Rabbit, to run the.—To convey liquor from a public-house.

Rag, to chew the.—To grieve; to brood.

Rag, to sky the.—To throw a towel into the air in token of surrender (pugilism).

Rain, to keep out of the.—To avoid danger; to act with caution.

Rat.—A street urchin; a wharf loafer.

Rattled.—Excited; confused.

Red 'ot.—Extreme; out-and-out.

Registry.—The office of a Registrar.

Ribuck.—Correct, genuine; an interjection signifying assent.

Rile.—To annoy. Riled.—Roused to anger.

Ring, the.—The arena of a prize-fight

Ring, the dead.—A remarkable likeness.

Rise, a.—An accession of fortune; an improvement.

Rocks.—A locality in Sydney.

Rorty.—Boisterous; rowdy.

Roust, or Rouse.—To upbraid with many words.

'Roy.—Fitzroy, a suburb of Melbourne; its football team.

Run against.—To meet more or less unexpectedly.

Saints.—A football team of St. Kilda, Victoria,

Sandy blight.—Ophthalmia.

Savvy.—Common-sense; shrewdness.

School.—A club; a clique of gamblers, or others.

Scran.—Food.

Scrap.—Fight.

Set, to.—To attack; to regard with disfavour.

Set, to have.—To have marked down for punishment or revenge.

Shick, shickered.—Intoxicated.

Shicker.—Intoxicating liquor.

Shinty.—A game resembling hockey.

Shook.—Stolen; disturbed.

Shook, on.—Infatuated.

Shyin' or Shine.—Excellent; desirable.

Sight.—To tolerate; to permit; also to see; observe.

Sir Garneo.—In perfect order; satisfactory.

Sky the wipe.—See "Rag."

Skirt or bit of skirt.—A female.

Skite.—To boast. Skiter.—A boaster

Slab.—A portion; a tall, awkward fellow.

Slanter.—Spurious; unfair.

Slap-up.—Admirable; excellent.

Slats.—The ribs.

Slaver.—One engaged in the "white slave traffic."

Slick.—Smart; deft; quick.

Slope, to.—To elope; to leave in haste.

Sloppy.—Lachrymose; maudlin.

Slushy.—A toiler in a scullery.

Smooge.—To flatter or fawn; to bill and coo.

Smooger.—A sycophant; a courtier.

Snag.—A hindrance; formidable opponent.

Snake-'eaded.—Annoyed; vindictive.

Snake juice.—Strong drink.

Snare.—To acquire; to seize; to win.

Snide.—Inferior; of no account.

Snob.—A bootmaker.

Snout.—To bear a grudge.

Snouted.—Treated with disfavour.

Snuff, or snuff it.—To expire.

Sock it into.—To administer physical punishment.

Solid.—Severe; severely.

So-long.—A form of farewell.

Sool.—To attack; to urge on.

Soot, leadin'.—A chief attribute.

Sore, to get.—To become aggrieved.

Sore-head.—A curmudgeon.

Sour, to turn, or get.—To become pessimistic or discontented.

Spank.—To chastise maternal-wise.

Spar.—A gentle bout at fisticuffs.

Spare me days.—A pious ejaculation.

Specs.—Spectacles.

Splash.—To expend.

Splice.—To join in matrimony.

Spout.—To preach or speak at length.

Sprag.—To accost truculently.

Spruik.—To deliver a speech, as a showman.

Square.—Upright, honest.

Square an' all.—Of a truth; verily.

Squiz.—A brief glance.

Stand-orf.—Retiring; reticent.

Stajum.—Stadium, where prize-fights are conducted.

Stiffened.—Bought over.

Stiff-un.—A corpse.

Stoke.—To nourish; to eat.

Stop a pot.—To quaff ale.

Stoush.—To punch with the fist. s. Violence.

Straight, on the.—In fair and honest fashion.

Strangle-hold.—An ungentle embrace in wrestling.

Strength of it.—The truth of it; the value of it.

Stretch, to do a.—To serve a term of imprisonment.

Strike.—The innocuous remnant of a hardy curse.

Strike.—To discover; to meet.

Strong, going.—Proceeding with vigour.

'Struth.—An emaciated oath.

Stuff.—Money.

Stunt.—A performance; a tale.

Swad, Swaddy.—A private soldier.

Swank.—Affectation; ostentation.

Swap.—To exchange.

Swell.—An exalted person.

Swig.—A draught of water or other liquid.

Tabbie.—A female.

Take 'em on.—Engage them in battle.

Take it out.—To undergo imprisonment in lieu of a fine.

Tart.—A young woman (contraction of sweetheart).

Tenner.—A ten-pound note.

Time, to do.—To serve a term in prison.

Time, to have no time for.—To regard with impatient disfavour.

Tip.—To forecast; to give; to warn.

Tip.—A warning; a prognostication; a hint.

Tipple.—Strong drink; to indulge in strong drink.

Toff.—An exalted person.

Togs.—Clothes.

Togged.—Garbed.

Tom.—A girl.

Tony.—Stylish.

Took.—Arrested; apprehended.

Top, off one's.—Out of one's mind.

Top off, to.—To knock down; to assault.

Touch.—Manner; mode; fashion.

Toss in the towel.—See "Rag."

Tough.—Unfortunate; hardy; also a "tug." q.v.

Tough luck.—Misfortune.

Track with.—To woo; to "go walking with."

Treat, a.—Excessively; abundantly.

Tucked away.—Interred.

Tug.—An uncouth fellow; a hardy rogue.

Tumble to, or to take a tumble.—To comprehend suddenly.

Turkey, head over.—Heels over head.

Turn down.—To reject; to dismiss.

Turn, out of one's.—Impertinently; uninvited.

Twig.—To observe; to espy.

Two-up School.—A gambling den.

Umpty.—An indefinite numeral.

Upper-cut.—In pugilism, an upward blow.

Uppish.—Proud.

Up to us.—Our turn; our duty.

Vag, on the.—Under the provisions of the Vagrancy Act.

Wallop.—To beat; chastise.

Waster.—A reprobate; an utterly useless and unworthy person.

Waterworks, to turn on the.—To shed tears.

Welt.—A blow.

Wet, to get.—To become incensed; ill-tempered.

Whips.—Abundance.

White (white man).—A true, sterling fellow.

White-headed boy.—A favourite; a pet.

Willin'.—Strenuous; hearty.

Win, a.—Success.

Wise, to get.—To comprehend; to unmask deceit.

Wolf.—To eat.

Word.—To accost with fair speech.

Wot price.—Behold; how now!

Yakker.—Hard Toil.

Yap.—To talk volubly.

Yowling.—Wailing; caterwauling.

About the Author

Clarence Michael James Dennis was born on 7 September 1876, the eldest son of an hotelier, at Auburn in the Clare Valley, South Australia. He began his career in the late 1890s, working as a journalist for the Adelaide weekly newspaper *The Critic*, and in 1903 he published his first poem "Urry' in *The Bulletin*. From February 1906, Dennis teamed up with A.E. Martin to edit and publish the weekly newspaper *The Gadfly*, which he left in 1907 when he moved to Melbourne. His 1908 poem 'A Real Australian Austra-laise' was awarded a special prize in a competition run by the *Bulletin*, and in early 1913 Dennis published his first volume of verse, *Backblock Ballads and Other Verses*, collected mainly from his earlier work on *The Critic* and *The Gadfly*. The book was not a financial or critical success.

In 1914 Dennis travelled to Sydney where he found work with the unionist journals *The Call* and *The Australian Worker*. His hard-drinking and dissolute lifestyle in Sydney took its toll, however, and he returned to Melbourne in September 1914, where he found work as a clerk at the Navy Office. In 1915, the Sydney firm of Angus & Robertson published a series of his poems in book form as *The Songs of a Sentimental Bloke*. The book was wildly successful and transformed Dennis virtually overnight into the most successful poet in Australia.

His next publication, *The Moods of Ginger Mick* (1916), was also a great success, and in 1917 Dennis followed it with *Doreen*. None of Dennis's publications after 1917 met with anything like the success of *The Songs of a Sentimental Bloke* and *The Moods of Ginger Mick*, but these two works were enough to establish his reputation as 'the laureate of the larrikin', and to provide him with a measure of financial stability. In July 1917,

Dennis married Olive Price and over the following years, spent a great deal of time extending the house and garden at Toolangi, outer Melbourne, which he nicknamed 'Arden'.

Dennis continued to publish new work, meeting with various degrees of success. He joined the staff of the Melbourne *Herald* in 1922, where his role as 'staff poet' would occupy the bulk of his creative energies for the rest of his life. According to his wife, the residence in Melbourne demanded by the *Herald* position exacerbated Dennis's drinking problem, and his health deteriorated. Dennis died of a heart condition brought on by asthma on 22 June 1938.

Select Bibliography of the Published Works of C.J. Dennis

Backblock Ballads and Other Verses. Melbourne: E.W. Cole, 1913.

The Songs of a Sentimental Bloke. Sydney: Angus & Robertson, 1915.

The Moods of Ginger Mick. Sydney: Angus & Robertson, 1916.

The Glugs of Gosh. Sydney: Angus & Robertson, 1917.

Doreen. Sydney: Angus & Robertson, 1917.

Digger Smith. Sydney: Angus & Robertson, 1918.

Jim of the Hills: A Story in Rhyme. Sydney: Angus & Robertson, 1919.

A Book for Kids. Sydney: Angus & Robertson, 1921.

Rose of Spadgers: A Sequel to "Ginger Mick". Sydney: Cornstalk Publishing, 1924.

"I Dips Me Lid" to the Sydney Harbor Bridge. Rhodes, New South Wales: L. Berger, 1932.

The Singing Garden. Sydney: Angus & Robertson, 1935.

Selected Verse of C.J. Dennis, edited by Alec H. Chisholm, Sydney: Angus & Robertson, 1950.

Random Verse: a collection of verse and prose by C.J. Dennis, sel. Margaret Herron, Melbourne: Hallcraft, 1952.

The C.J. Dennis Collection: from his 'forgotten' writings, edited by Garrie Hutchinson, Melbourne: Lothian, 1987.

The Ant Explorer. South Melbourne: Macmillan, 1988

Hist! Montville, Queensland: Walter McVitty Books, 1991.

Other Titles in the Australian Classics Library Series

Jessica Anderson, *The Commandant,* ISBN 9781920898946

Barbara Baynton, *Bush Studies,* ISBN 9781920898953

Martin Boyd, *A Difficult Young Man,* ISBN 9781920898960

Rosa Cappiello, *Oh Lucky Country,* ISBN 9781920898977

Ernest Favenc, *Tales of the Austral Tropics,* ISBN 9781920898991

William Lane, *The Workingman's Paradise,* ISBN 9781920899004

Henry Lawson, *Joe Wilson and His Mates,* ISBN 9781920899011

Gerald Murnane, *Inland,* ISBN 9781920899028

A.B. Paterson, *The Man from Snowy River and Other Verses,* ISBN 9781920899035

Henry Handel Richardson, *Maurice Guest,* ISBN 9781920899042

Price Warung, *Tales of the Early Days,* ISBN: 9781920899059

For further information and a complete list of books published by Sydney University Press please see our website at sydney.edu.au/sup